How We Came to Be

Praise for How We Came to Be

How We Came to Be is a story of the ties that bind us to one another. It is a story of testing how far those ties can be strained without breaking, and of how the least expected connections we make become the ones that sustain us. Bernhard's writing style is a wonderful blend of witty and poignant that makes her characters come to life.
—Megan Holt, Executive Director, One Book One New Orleans

A Must Read
—*Southern Writers Magazine*, March/April 2018 issue

Bernhard weaves a rapid-fired contemporary narrative with characters we all can recognize and cheer on. Added to the rich tapestry of broken lives and tangled dilemmas is the joy of seeing the characters answer the three questions Jesus Christ asked those seeking His miracles of healing: what do you want? where do you hurt? do you want to be healed?
—Sarah Cortez, award-winning author/editor of *Vanishing Points* and *Tired, Hungry, and Standing in One Spot for Twelve Hours: Essential Cop Essays*

Johnnie Bernhard is at the top of her game in her second novel, *How We Came to Be*, a midlife coming of age tale narrated by a high school English teacher with a big heart, enough spunk and witty one-liners to keep readers turning the page. With her penchant for nightly glasses of wine, her worry over her adoptive college-age daughter, Tiffany, and her new friendship with an elderly neighbor across the street, Karen Anders is the kind of narrator women can relate to and root for. We weep when Karen weeps and we laugh when she laughs. We curl up with her and her dog, Max, and her cat, Poncho, and long to find our place in the world. Well written, gorgeous, straight forward prose told in a conversational style that pulls you right in, this novel feels like sitting down with a friend. This is a novel for women who have a passion for witty and wise characters and who aren't afraid to cheer for the downtrodden and the forgotten in life.
—Kathleen M. Rodgers, award-winning author of *The Final Salute*, *Johnnie Come Lately*, and *Seven Wings to Glory*.

Johnnie Bernhard, through a colorful weaving of wit, wisdom, tears and faith, crafts an intriguing novel of coming of age for the twenty-first century family.

—Larry Massey, 1430 AM Houston-Catholic radio personality and Podcast Host of HoustonAlive.org

On the heels of her successful literary novel, *A Good Girl*, Johnnie Bernhard has scored yet another win with *How We Came to Be*.

—Jim Fraiser, Book Reviewer for *The Sun Herald* and author of *Shadow Seed*, and *The French Quarter of New Orleans*

Bernhard writes with the ease of someone who can walk a mile in her characters' shoes, and I promise you'll fall in love with Tiffany, Karen and the rest of her cast as they humorously navigate life's joys and struggles.

—Erin Z. Bass, Editor of *Deep South Magazine*

How We Came to Be

JOHNNIE BERNHARD

Texas Review Press
Huntsville, Texas

FIRST EDITION
Requests for permission to acknowledge material from this work should be sent to:

> Permissions
> Texas Review Press
> English Department
> Sam Houston State University
> Huntsville, TX 77341-2146

ACKNOWLEDGMENTS:
A special thank you to Sharon and Joe Ely for permission to use the lyrics from "All Just to Get to You" and New Directions Publishing for permis-sion to use William Carlos Williams' poem, "The Red Wheelbarrow."

Cover Art by Nancy Parsons
Cover Design by Nancy Parsons
Author Photograph by Valerie Winn

Library of Congress Cataloging-in-Publication Data
Names: Bernhard, Johnnie, 1962- author.
Title: How we came to be / Johnnie Bernhard.
Description: Huntsville, Texas : Texas Review Press, [2018] |
Identifiers: LCCN 2018002046 (print) | LCCN 2018004161 (ebook) | ISBN
    9781680031577 (ebook) | ISBN 9781680031560 | ISBN 9781680031560¬q(pbk.)
Subjects: LCSH: High school teachers--Houston--Texas--Fiction. | Single
    mothers--Houston--Texas--Fiction. | Middle-aged
    mothers--Houston--Texas--Fiction.
Classification: LCC PS3602.E75966 (ebook) | LCC PS3602.E75966 H69 2018
    (print) | DDC 813/.6--dc23
LC record available at https://lccn.loc.gov/2018002046

For Single Mothers

THAT crazed girl improvising her music.
Her poetry, dancing upon the shore,

Her soul in division from itself
Climbing, falling She knew not where,
Hiding amid the cargo of a steamship,
Her knee-cap broken, that girl I declare
A beautiful lofty thing, or a thing
Heroically lost, heroically found.

No matter what disaster occurred
She stood in desperate music wound,
Wound, wound, and she made in her triumph
Where the bales and the baskets lay
No common intelligible sound
But sang, "O sea-starved, hungry sea."

—W. B. Yeats

How We Came to Be

Chapter One
My Brother's Keeper

Parenting is a life sentence without parole. Wine makes it tolerable. Like millions of middle-aged single parents, I took my daily shot of courage without remorse. I wasn't fighting cavities like my mother's generation. I was in full-scale combat with social media trolls and tattoo parlors serving eighteen-year-olds. By the second glass of Pinot Noir, I found the nerve to ask her.

"Why did you tattoo the date your dad died on your wrist?"

"I want to remember that day for the rest of my life."

"You really need permanent ink to remind you?"

Tiffany was preparing to leave the nest and launch herself into the adult world. I was preparing to redefine that nest I created in 1997 when her father, my only brother, dropped dead of a heart attack in front of the mail box. In Danny's hands were the bills from the plastic surgeon who performed the breast augmentation on his ex-wife, Sherry.

I wish I could give those dark days a glimmer of light. None existed in Houston with the economy choked by OPEC and yet another war in the Middle East. When oil plummeted to less than $20 a barrel; all hell broke loose in the form of pink slips, foreclosures, and divorces.

Things haven't changed much since then. Just like the great recession of 2008, the Eighties recession made every three-two box slapped together suburban home mortgaged at eighteen percent interest a spreading cancer until Southwest Houston became a ghost town.

My brother tried to keep the marriage together in the beginning. He and Sherry picked up the pieces and walked out of their dream home in Houston, taking their six-foot privacy fence, mini blinds, and dishwasher with them. They piled it in the back of a Chevy Suburban and headed toward a place of lowered expectations and cheaper rent. My brother got a job making a fourth of what he had made. Fragile and unwanted, Tiffany came into the world several years later and was placed in a crib next to the bed of Sherry and Danny in a $500-a-month apartment overlooking I-10.

It was not the life Sherry dreamed of, so she found a plastic surgeon who took installment payments for a D cup and vaginal rejuvenation surgery. She then test drove her improvements with Barry Holly, a former Houston cop turned full-time body builder.

Their first business venture, outside of being husband and wife, was HOT TUB EMPORIUM of Houston. Instead of a dot above the *i* in emporium, there was a red-hot flashing heart. With a clever logo and business model, Sherry and Barry rented hot tubs by the hour in a cavern of a building, complete with a liquor license and an assortment of flavored oils.

Sherry and Barry were soon making money hand over fist and opened HOT TUB EMPORIUM II on Canal Street in New Orleans. But their success was short-lived. The fear of STDs and lawsuits lingered far longer than the scent of disinfectants.

In a few months, the pair was back on their feet. They opened a Pilates studio and a paddle board rental in Kailua, Oahu. Sherry taught middle-aged, overweight women how to breathe properly during private sessions on the Pilates Reformer, while Barry kept middle-aged, overweight men from drowning in the Pacific while paddle boarding. Apparently, there's a lot of money in those fields. They never moved back to Texas, and Sherry never asked to have her daughter back.

That pretty much sums it up. That's how I got Tiffany. It is the one single thing in my life I have never regretted. I am my brother's keeper, who happens to also be an average high school English teacher challenged by the terrors of daily drinking.

Average is not a negative word for me. I'm average weight and height, relative to the ten-pound spread that comes and goes with the holidays. The forehead isn't sloped, but the nose isn't perfectly straight. I'm somewhere between the girl next door and the class clown. No over-achiever here. There's a lot of comfort in being dead center.

On my tombstone, it will read, "Average English teacher who drank daily." Nothing more. Nothing less. But late at night, when all I hear is my heart beating against my chest, I allow myself to feel, to think, to pray. I remember my real job. I am Tiffany's adopted mother and father rolled into one. I'm all she's got.

Like millions of mothers and daughters around the world, we've arrived to the pivotal moment in our relationship. Tiffany is gaining her independence and I'm floundering in an empty nest. It's just like the false excitement of her high school graduation ceremony, infested with Mylar balloons and people packed into bleachers. I'm hating every moment, but pretending it's the time of my life. My gut says the transition will be hell, but I tamp that down with a bottle of wine. What I can't escape is the simple heartbreaking fact, she's all I've got.

Chapter Two
Promised Land

"Karen, did you throw out my magazines?"

"You didn't really want to move a five-year stack of magazines covered in cat hair to Austin? For God's sake, I did you a favor."

"They're mine. You had no right to throw them out, no right to even go in my room."

For Tiffany, the written word was sacred. She was either writing or telling the world about its responsibility to protect it since she won the Voice of Democracy essay sponsored by the South Texas Veterans of Foreign Wars in the eighth grade. She received a blue ribbon and a check for fifty dollars in a Kodak memory of her wedged between me and a Vietnam veteran with one-arm. The essay prize was complete with a complimentary chicken fried steak dinner at the VFW hall, following a passionate singing of "God Bless America."

For a child who didn't begin speaking, not even a babble or goo, until she was three, she wasted no time in making up for it. Every hour of every day, she let the world know who she was, where she was going, and what her inalienable rights were. She and her cell phone were a 24-7 cable news outlet. Whether it was worth reporting or not, she was going to tell her story.

As for me, I didn't have any rights, only responsibilities. Go to work, pay the bills.

To avoid yet another explosive argument, I said nothing.

Best to let her ramble on, so she'll sleep during the drive to Austin, and I could begin dealing with my empty nest in peace. Let me count the ways I will enjoy it!

Tiffany was accepted into the University of Texas after applying the beginning of her senior year at Heights Central High School. I begged her to apply to a smaller school. It just made sense to attend a school with a student body count of 25,000 or less. That first year away from home was hard enough without the added stress of being lost in a crowd.

Tiffany ignored my reasoning. She loved the idea of a huge state university and being lost in the crowd. Who would design such a platform for learning? Here's a recipe for a free-for-all: put 52,000 people between the ages of eighteen and thirty living within a five-mile radius of each other and let 'er rip!

Her reason for attending UT was disturbing to me, but I kept it to myself. It was as if she were saying, "I know I'm not beautiful; I know I'm not rich, and I know my mother doesn't want me, so I chose to be alternative and Austinized." It pained me she was filled with such self-doubt. Social trends became a way to reinvent herself; anything was better than being the child her mother didn't want. I watched her insecurities manifest themselves throughout her childhood in various ways–bed wetting, nail biting and the refraining chorus, "Why don't they like me?"

I wish I could get my hands on the man who wrote, *Keep Austin Weird*. I heard it made him a millionaire, and he and his money moved to a retiree village of hippies and hipsters on Lake Travis. All his moniker did was make it okay to give up on any standard or routine, everything a kid with a broken heart and a crazy family needed to make it in life. It began a marching tune for the naïve and young looking for acceptance in a place that offered it all.

Tiffany would probably come out of UT $50,000 in debt with a bachelor's in social-pseudo-liberal arts for a promising career in the service industry.

That's the game change the shifting economy made certain. No guarantees. The days of a great job for even the stupid and lazy were over forever when Jimmy Carter handed Ronald Reagan the gavel. It's been trickle down middle class ever since.

The one time I made the mistake of offering career advice was in the form of the very humble yet practical teaching certificate.

"Are you kidding me?" She exploded. "I've not met one public school teacher in twelve years who has job satisfaction written on her face."

"It's an insurance policy, Tiffany. You'll always have a job."

"Don't stifle my creativity, Karen."

"Right. The world is begging for more twenty-two-year-olds with liberal arts degrees in obscure subjects."

"Karen; it's my life; you've had the chance to live yours," she said, slamming the door to emphasize the point that at fifty, I was no longer standing on terra firma.

She thought Austin was the promise land of freedom and artistic creativity. But how can a fifty-year-old woman, divorced, in a mediocre career have credibility with an eighteen-year-old? On the rare occasions I would warn her about the hook up culture, it would take her two minutes to put me in my place.

"What? Are we going to discuss the birds and the bees? I'm out there every day living in the culture. I think I have a better understanding of what a hook up is compared to you. You've spent the last fifteen years hiding in this house and in your classroom. I'm the one who should be counseling you." Then right on cue, she'd slam the bedroom door.

So, I gave up and ramped up my nightly wine ration from two to three glasses the final year she lived with me.

I had been a good parent to Tiffany, loving her more than anyone I would ever love. I gave her stability. I kept the two-bedroom, one-bath bungalow I bought with my ex in the Heights. It was a classic 1910 block-and-beam foundation with a front porch. I loved the house more than I loved my ex. That divorce was one of the easiest things I ever did in my life. When Greg deemed my career as a high school teacher raising a mute a stumbling block to personal happiness, I checked him off as a bad mistake from the get go.

The first sign it was over was when he wanted to sell the bungalow and move to a McMansion suburban hell off the Katy Freeway. His boss lived there and had invited us to a progressive dinner party. I still don't know where the word progressive came from, because we never left the house for the next course. We stayed at the boss man's pseudo Italian villa, complete with garden gnomes guarding the front door.

That was the night that marked the end of our marriage. Maybe the only progressive thing about that dinner event was my state of mind. It was as if the cosmos aligned and showed me a parade of red flags of why I shouldn't be married to Greg. The first red flag was Greg's good-natured chuckle at the garden gnomes leading us to the twelve-foot wood and black iron forged door. The second gosh darn moment came seconds later when the boss' wife Pamela greeted us at the front door wearing a leopard print jumpsuit with matching pumps. Greg looked at her with the admiration of a layman observing the Mona Lisa. I saw it. I felt it in the pit of my stomach. I knew then I could never be what he wanted.

The rest of the night I bullied his boss into pouring an endless supply of Bordeaux as Pamela gave us the house tour, complete with a collection of faux Fabergé eggs tucked in miniature stiletto pumps in the china cabinet and an accent wall dedicated to Hummel figurines. The final tour item of interest was the bidet with LED lights. The little tour group squealed with delight at the glow-in-the-dark FLUSH control.

I knew I would never fit in that world. I'd have to be a full-time drunk to run in that crowd. Every time I looked at Greg that night to gauge his interest, his face glowed with delight. My ex loved it, *just* loved it.

I didn't shed too many tears watching him go. I had a toddler, a dog, a cat, and a full-time teaching job. There just wasn't any time to feel sorry for myself. In fact, the thought of no longer seeing him dressed in matching suspenders and tie for his day in court made me giddy. The entire house breathed a sigh of relief when he left.

I still love the house, but like all things you love, they come at a great price to keep. It needed pressure washing, scraping, and painting almost yearly in the humid-heat gunk of Houston. It needed new plumbing and wiring. It was a lot of money on a teacher's salary. I did most of it myself or hired Carl, a science teacher I worked with, who did the complicated stuff in the summer.

My single mom budget centered on chicken leg quarters, diapers, and child care. The advice I received from my married friends was to clip coupons and buy in bulk. In order to use the coupon, I had to buy luxury items like name brand ketchup and toilet paper. Buying in bulk required cash, real cash. Dual income families and their budgeting credo was light-years away from my reality, the life of a single, working mother.

My single friends, whether divorced with children or divorced and childless, there's a moniker to keep you awake at night, became my family. A vacation was in the backyard with a plastic kiddie pool and a grill lined with hot dogs. There were day trips to Galveston with plastic pails and shovels, and sandwiches wrapped in wax paper. The splurge would be ice cream cones for the ride home, after we cleaned the bottom of our feet with lighter fluid, removing tar from the latest oil spill in Galveston Bay. As dreary as it sounded, there was nothing sweeter than to bathe Tiffany once we were home. Her body was pink from a day in the sun. The strawberry blond hair, curly and wild with sand and water, appeared as a halo above her tiny brown eyes.

While I massaged her back with a soapy wash cloth, she lined the edge of the bathtub with sea shells she had found that day. Each one was carefully selected by her perfect hands.

So, I made a life for us. Taking care of the house and teaching was a schedule an abandoned child could heal in. It never bothered me. I never felt like I was giving anything up to raise her. It was a big life. It was enough for me.

Now, at eighteen, Tiffany wanted her own life. Frankly, I thought the separation was the best thing for my mental health. Between her butterfly tattoo on the lower back, the current one on her wrist, the belly button piercing with the pink diamond, a parade of crazy boyfriends and unending drama with her girl-friends, we had reached a stand-off. The final blow came the last semester of her senior year.

Menopause and all its glory was hanging on with hot flashes, facial hair, and insomnia, while Tiffany's monthly cycle came with big, ugly cries and door slamming around the clock every twenty-eight days. It was too much for a two-bedroom house; there wasn't room for escape. I'd either kill her in her sleep or she'd poison me at breakfast. Both of us were on edge.

Max, my seven-year-old Border Collie who was controlled by slices of processed cheese, slept through most of the fighting. The only sane one in the house was Poncho, an overweight, grey cat with an extra digit on his paw. Even Poncho became part of our arguments.

"Stop overfeeding Poncho," Tiffany would scream from the kitchen each morning before leaving for school.

"How do you know I'm overfeeding him?"

"Look at his waistline—gone!"

"Cats don't have waistlines."

"That's right, Karen. Make him a clone of you. You're killing Poncho. Stop it now."

"Got it. Have a good day at school."

The reason I overfed Poncho was guilt. I felt sorry for him, living in that mad house with two crazy women and a dog who slept his life away.

Two months before high school graduation, Tiffany did the unthinkable.

She painted "*faber est suae quisque fortunae*" on her bedroom ceiling in large black letters. I shook violently as I Googled the interpretation, "Every human is the artisan of her own fortune." For God's sake. It was a dagger in my heart. I dedicated my very existence to the historic integrity of that house—all abandoned in a thirty-minute rage from an eighteen-year-old.

Our nightly ritual became very simple after that. It always began and ended the same way.

"I love you, Aunt Karen, but you are driving me crazy."

The minute I heard the conjunction in any sentence she spoke, I knew there was more drama to come. And it always came in the form of a slamming door. I merely looked up from the kitchen table with a pile of badly written essays, giving her a quick glance to acknowledge her suffering, then grabbed a red ink pen and watched the white paper fill with *spelling! Incomplete sentence! No thesis! Improper subject verb agreement!* On and on, until I had emptied my third glass of wine. Bedtime!

But life would change for Tiffany and me, as it always does. It was the cruelest of jokes God played on us. We humans finally had a plan for living day to day, learning to buffer the disappointments, learning to forgive the unforgiveable, then suddenly, game change. In the wake, we reel from side to side, mouthing, "What am I supposed to do now?"

I had almost two decades to prepare for this day, and it still wasn't enough. Tiffany was off to Austin and God knows what else. Now, I could be the thoroughly lonely, divorced, average woman I always wanted to be. Sticky pad note to self: Tiffany *was not* taking Poncho with her.

Chapter Three
The Roar of Intended Silence

The first week without her was pure heaven. No slamming doors, no angry cries of indignation, and no waiting for late-night texts with the usual messages: "I'm spending the night at Gretchen's house." "I need a ride NOW." "Jeep on empty. No dinero." "Flat tire, stranded in Montrose." I slept ten hours the first night she was gone.

The next morning, I cleaned the house listening to the radio, happy in the mindless task of scrubbing a toilet bowl and sweeping dog and cat hair from underneath the furniture. It had been years since I could concentrate on the job at hand without a witch's brew in my head of what ifs—where's the car, who's she with, why isn't she home . . . of course, I knew these things were taking place, but amazingly, the miles apart also distanced me from the responsibility.

It just felt good to be in my own skin. Just Karen. Not teacher, employee, aunt, taxpayer, just me alone. My head and body felt in sync. No tension headaches, no joint ache from overuse of my right hand to write, grade, and clean. No backache from standing in front of a classroom of students for eight hours. It felt good. Marvelous, even.

As I cleaned the house, I dragged a forty-gallon garbage bag behind me. Once I began sweeping underneath Tiffany's bed, the bag quickly filled.

I found several paper plates with pizza cheese microwaved

to them, odd socks, a Sudoku puzzle done in ink, and an empty pack of cigarettes. This sent me into a momentary rage. An hour later, her room was clean and the bag was full. In it symbolized things I couldn't change in the past, things I had to live with to maintain peace between an eighteen-year-old and me. Things I reminded her of constantly: no junk food, no cigarettes, and no slobs allowed.

Maybe I should view the next four years as our chance at a positive lifestyle change. We'd merge our well-educated, slimmer, sober selves into a new family. A better family, one where two mature women began each day with coffee and a smile of approval.

I just assumed her first week in college was a happy one. Meeting new people, enjoying dorm life. My Tiffany was reading and writing her way to fiscal responsibility.

While we hadn't spoken much in the first week, we did communicate in short pithy texts: "K! 2moro! B4N! BCNU!"

By the beginning of the second week, I needed to hear her voice. For three days, I left voice messages without a single text or returned phone call. I imagined the worst with each new message I left.

"Tiffany, give me a call not a text. I need to hear your voice." This was the first message. Thirty minutes later, I left this on her voicemail, "Have you been kidnapped?"

After eating half a pizza standing at the kitchen sink, crazed with anxiety, I called and left this message, "If you don't call me by 8:00 p.m., I'm contacting the RA in your dorm." That last message did it, because my phone rang fifteen minutes before 8:00 p.m.

"Hey. I've just been really busy with school."

"That's great, honey. How's things going? I'm most curious about your lit class? Maybe you can share a few things with me, so I know if I'm preparing my kids at school."

"It's pretty bad. The professor is an old man who reads poetry out loud to us and stares at the open window after each stanza. Once people sign in for attendance, the exodus begins. All the prof does is sigh and read another line of poetry."

"That's too bad. What are you reading?"

"The usual."

Time to switch topics, I thought.

"Hey, are you meeting anyone?"

"Yeah. Going to a mixer on Thursday night."

"A mixer—at a frat house? I didn't think you were entertaining the Greek Life?"

"I'm not. It's a free party. My roommate and I are going."

"Who's your roommate?"

"That's enough with the questions, Karen. This is supposed to be a conversation, not an interrogation. My roommate is from Memorial. She's a writer."

"Oh." What I wanted to say was how original for a rich white girl to write soul-wrenching prose while sitting cross legged in a dorm at UT. Instead I gave a weak "That's great."

"I'm running low on cash. I didn't think things would be this expensive. "

"Sure, I'll transfer some money over for you. You know, it might be helpful to keep a tab of all your expenses. Just write down what you spend in a notebook. Makes you think before you spend."

"If it's too much to get a couple of hundred together for me, forget it. I'll get a job."

"No, no. Your job is to go to school. I was just saying . . . well, forget it. I'm glad you called. I miss you, Tiff. Poncho and Max miss you, too."

"Hey, well. Bye."

And she was gone.

Chapter Four
A Thoroughly Modern Woman

November arrived with plastic pumpkins and cornucopia from China hot-glued to every door in the neighborhood. All around me were symbols of gratitude, brotherhood, and sharing. What I saw was another reason China owned us, and I was behind the eight ball in getting my plastic crap up on my front door. What was wrong with just having a nice meal for Thanksgiving? When did it turn into every other holiday, where the decorations were more important than the event? Time to suck it up, get in the attic, and haul down my collection of plastic. Sticky pad note to self: buy some pumpkin-shaped orange mini-lights for the front porch.

I began November in a foul mood. What I didn't know then was how it would go from foul to meltdown in a year. If I could put a label on that first year Tiffany was gone, it would be "Unchartered waters, mind your speed." Instead, we both cried, "Full speed ahead." Oh, the damage we left in that wake.

The warning signs were there. I ignored every one of them. She and I continued to communicate mostly by two-syllable texts and a weekend phone conversation of no more than five minutes. Neither one of us seemed to care.

With Tiffany gone, I increased my drinking each night. I don't know how it happened. It just did. The cut-off mark of three glasses somehow got to four, then on the weekends, to an entire bottle a night. It depended on how hard I worked on the weekend, really. If I mowed the yard, painted a wall, or mopped a floor, I felt entitled to a pain-free outlet. I justified it by telling myself I cleaned my own house; I mowed my own yard; I ironed my own clothes, and still put in a sixty-hour week with teaching, grading papers, and listening to angry parents and students. It was better than taking painkillers or aspirin when my middle-aged joints screamed in protest. I always had a way of justifying my behavior.

Once the Bordeaux got too expensive, I abandoned my quality not quantity mantra and switched to Pinky's Wine of the Week, available at Pinky's Discount Liquor, conveniently located next to my favorite grocery store.

Pinky's Wine of the Week replaced that lovely little French cork with a screw-on cap for a Chilean Syrah that coated my stomach and brain with a sticky, thick blackberry, black pepper wash. A red flag furled in my direction of what was to come and it arrived in headaches, sour stomach, and a bad disposition.

The next fail safe I initiated that fall was to buy smaller wine glasses. I had read an article in *O Magazine!* about the illusion of using smaller plates and glasses as a means of decreasing your portion size. You had to hand it to Oprah, she was still trying to save the middle class from its own demise.

I thought I'd start with downsizing the wine glasses. I dropped off the fish bowls on a stem at Goodwill one Saturday. Next door was a Tuesday Morning. I purchased four little glasses with Monarch butterflies gliding across the glass. Cute. It was so easy I almost thought it was Divine Intervention.

Feeling confident and in control, I agreed to do something I rarely did when Tiffany was at home. I became social. Yes, I purchased a weekend wardrobe with fun custom jewelry the day I placed a social calendar app on my phone. When I heard that little beep, a feeling of well-being flooded my brain. I was meeting friends in Rice Village for drinks and appetizers after work. It was a great weekend routine, for a while.

Friday evening found me preparing for Happy Hour at Fergal's Irish Pub. Between loads of laundry and checking my voice mail on the landline, I sent Tiffany a text. Rarely did I hear her voice, but I came to accept that a text was better than nothing.

"How r u?" I texted my usual Friday evening message.

"Coming home for TK," she replied.

"Great! It will be the best," I replied, laughing to myself. I could hardly believe she broke the ice first. It would be a great Thanksgiving for us; we'd make the cornbread dressing together, do some shopping, find a Christmas tree, and watch movies on the couch with Poncho and Max. I was so pleased with the possibilities; I was smiling at myself in the bathroom mirror as I applied mascara and eyeshadow for my evening out with friends.

Fergal's Irish Pub offered $3 Guinness and .25 cent wings on Friday till 7:00 p.m. I never got the Guinness and wing combo, but Carl lived for those Friday nights at Fergal's. Kelly, an English II teacher who taught in the classroom next door to me for twenty-three years, always joined us.

Carl and Kelly made our little threesome in the pub tolerable. At least the conversation was elevated to functional literate. These people wrote complete sentences and used more than two syllables when speaking. I loved teaching and my students, but by Friday I needed to be with adults, adults who were also friends.

Carl was the first to pen us as the three lucky charms: divorced, happily single, and aching to retire. We also were closet Catholics. Our divorces made us "those Catholics." I couldn't quite get over the fact that my marriage lacked anything close to God's idea of a man and woman becoming one.

We were immature when we stood at the altar in front of our families and friends, making a vow to support each other, regardless, until death ended the marriage. But worse than that, we were selfish. I wanted what I wanted, and Greg wanted what he wanted. Selfish and the penalty for that was loneliness.

I was a church outcast, loser in a sacrament. I still tried to make it to Mass, every now and then. I craved the peace it gave me. But I didn't talk about that too much, especially with Carl and Kelly.

Besides, an Irish pub was for telling Catholic jokes, and the three of us usually tried to outdo each other. The wit meter on those Friday nights hovered in the self-proclaimed brilliant range by the third round.

"I've got a good one for tonight," said Carl.

"Oh yeah?" I leaned in to the table to hear him.

"An Irish priest is driving in Galway and gets stopped for speeding. The guard smells alcohol on the priest's breath and then sees an empty wine bottle on the floor of the car. He says, 'Father, have you been drinking?' 'Just water,' says the priest. The guard replies, 'Then why do I smell wine?' The priest looks at the bottle and says, 'Good Lord! He's done it again!'"

"Good one!" Kelly laughed. "For a moment there I actually forgot about the crappy day I had." Kelly Sparing, a forty-nine-year-old with legs like two pillars of chiseled marble that began from the tattered strings of a too-short, too-tight pair of Levi shorts and ended in a pair of black Lucchese boots, was rarely in a bad mood. The black tank top she was wearing screamed, "YOU CAN'T SPELL TRUTH WITHOUT RUTH." A headshot of Ruth Bader Ginsburg was centered underneath the slogan.

"What happened, Kelly?" I offered, as I watched Carl crunch the wings of chickens dipped in blue cheese from the corner of my eyes.

"It was the mandatory dress code check in first hour. Apparently, I let a kid slip from my class to second hour wearing a ripped tee shirt that exposed the red bra she was wearing," Kelly replied.

"Well, what that all means is the second hour teacher wasn't teaching. She was practicing her watch as a Gestapo guard," I offered. "I bet the teacher who turned you and the kid in was that monster down the hall from me. You know, she teaches Algebra II."

"Cynthia Martin," offered Carl between bites of bone and charred chicken skin.

"Yeah, I bet it was her. That woman has worn the same pair of khaki slacks and polo shirt in either black, blue or coral since 2005. Who in the hell wears slacks in the second millennium?" Kelly asked.

"Yep. That's her. Still hating anyone with the imagination to rip a shirt as a fashion statement compared to the polyester-blend hazmat suit she wears every day," I finalized.

"When Kenny called me into his office to discuss my failure

to reinforce the dress code, there was a copy of the student handbook on his desk," continued Kelly.

"And. . . ," said Carl.

"He told me to turn to page twenty-eight and read."

"You're kidding," I added, all the while thinking to myself what a jerk Kenny Ramsey was as an assistant principal. He pulled himself up from the gathering of apes the coaching staff had become when online administration classes were offered. The students we shared said he never taught. He'd write the assignment on the board, "Read pages fifty-three through seventy-two and answer the questions at the end of the chapter." It got so bad by mid-term, he'd only erase and add new page numbers at the urging of the students. Of course, Kenny got his Master's in Supervision and Leadership while collecting a paycheck as an American History teacher.

"Kenny had already dogeared the page and highlighted in yellow what he wanted me to read from the student handbook, which tells me he has way too much time on his hands," said Kelly. "So, I read it slowly, 'Students should choose clothing as to reflect a neat and modest appearance while attending school.'"

"Oh no," I offered.

Carl looked directly at Kelly, waiting for the punchline. A pile of chicken bones and rejected celery sticks lay in his wake.

"The first thing out of Kenny's mouth was 'Ms. Sparing, why didn't you send Alisa Martinez to me when you saw the huge rip in her shirt and the red bra she was wearing?'"

"Because I didn't notice her ripped shirt or her red bra, Mr. Ramsey. I was too busy teaching twenty-seven tenth graders, who read on a fifth-grade level, how to interpret *Julius Caesar*. But I do have a question for you."

"Here it comes, folks," laughed Carl, cleansing his palate with a Guinness.

Kelly smiled at both of us with those enormous green eyes of hers, bursting with triumph.

"Mr. Ramsey, define neat and modest appearance for me. When you do, I might consider spending fifty minutes of instruction time enforcing it. By the way, I'm afraid you have a mustard stain near the third button of your shirt," Kelly said.

The three lucky charms exploded with laughter and ordered round two, which included Jameson chasers to top off the Guinness.

Following round three, I knew I was drunk when I got up to go to the restroom. It was probably close to nine o'clock; the crowd was changing from working professionals to the thirty-year-olds who had time to change from their work clothes to $80 shirts and expensive watches. The women's makeup and hair didn't have the appearance of being done in the car while in traffic at 7:00 a.m. on the way to work. Hair and makeup became serious for women in their thirties. They were gathered to find a suitable mate for the night.

When I was a kid, I first learned there wasn't a bit of difference between four-legged animals and two-legged animals, men and women, except that dogs are probably the closest to the saints in their ability to love unconditionally.

Prime time television in the late Sixties was *Mutual of Omaha's Wild Kingdom*. I watched it cross-legged on the living room floor. A barrel-shaped, lovely old man with a beard would introduce each week's program, which included quite a bit of footage of animals during the mating season. To this day, I cannot lose the image of the elks parading in front of the females, puffed-up and rutting, occasionally locking horns. Then the host of *Mutual of Omaha's Wild Kingdom* would pronounce with perfect diction, "The formation and retention of the antlers is testosterone-driven, followed by an elevation in the level of pheromones during mating season."

Was that any different from a Houston bar on a Friday night, where women bathed themselves in perfume while men flexed their wallets and biceps? Get out on the dance floor, and the humans were making the same moves as the elks during mating season. It's quite a visual to keep locked in your head.

The dating scene at my age was no different. With testosterone shots and Viagra readily available, like hamburgers and fries in a drive-thru window, we were shaking our groove things until we dropped dead. Maybe that's why I was still single. Romance? I gave up on that years ago.

But I was having a great time at Fergal's Pub; in fact, one of the best I had in years, so despite being drunk, I cozied up to my friends at our little table near the dance floor, and that old familiar feeling of letting go and not caring spread throughout my body like a liquid blanket of warmth and confidence.

"What do you think about the *Call of the Wild* on the dance floor?" I said to Carl when I sat down.

"It's deadly serious. The ugly girls and the guys making minimum wage have gone home for the night or to the lower end of Westheimer. All that's left are the beautiful, seriously employed and their imaginations," laughed Carl. "I think we should join the fray."

"Kelly, are you still seeing that American History teacher? Jim? Was his name Jim?" I asked.

"Jim and I are no longer a couple. I don't play the game like people in their thirties do. I'm much too tired to go through all that pretense. The best way to get over a man is to get under another one. If I find someone I'm attracted to, I just let it out."

I laughed. "What do you mean, let it out?"

"I say, 'Hello, I'm Kelly. I'm bipolar and I've been married twice.' If the guy is still standing in front of me after that, I ask him if he'd like to get a drink."

"Right. No use in wasting time on formalities," I said. "Carl, flag the waitress. I need a glass of water."

"Quitter," he said.

"Maybe I should eat something, too."

"Do you want the celery sticks from my wings? There's still lots of blue cheese left," Carl offered.

"Come on," Kelly said. "Get up and dance a little. It will make you feel better."

I danced in a small circle with Carl and Kelly, until I became dizzy and nauseous. I stopped the spinning by grabbing Carl's shoulder.

"I'm going home. See you Monday morning," and with that

I was out the door, searching for my keys at the bottom of my purse and trying to remember where I parked the car.

I knew Houston well enough that I could take crossroads and drive through neighborhoods without getting on a main road back to the North Loop. I'd keep my speed down, the radio off, and both hands on the wheel. What I didn't take into consideration were the medians on Morningside Drive with their newly planted crepe myrtles.

I don't know how I did it. Maybe I turned too sharp. I probably overcompensated for the width of the street versus the cement curves of the medians. I took out three crepe myrtles before I swung hard to the left. I dragged the trees to Kirby Drive, where I found a gas station combination convenience store—food trough still open. Behind the store, I pulled the trees out of the wheel well, jumped back into the Jeep, and studied my rearview mirror for suspecting cops. I limped my way home with a pounding headache and the Jeep pulling to the right, because the alignment was shot to hell.

The last thing I remember was throwing my purse on the coffee table and wedging myself between Poncho and Max on the couch.

I got up Saturday morning and greeted myself in the mirror. I had a black eye. My head must have hit the steering wheel when the Jeep hit the curb. I spent the rest of the weekend Googling ways to camouflage a black eye.

There was no way I could go to school sporting a shiner. You couldn't fool a teacher or a student with under-eye coverage. We spent hours upon hours in after school trainings on child abuse. We knew the signs. And to think this black eye was self-inflicted. I would be the butt of endless jokes in the teacher's lounge. But the real problem would be in the classroom. I would lose my credibility with the kids. I couldn't handle that. It wasn't going to happen.

Apparently, concealing a black eye was a worldwide problem, because the websites and YouTube videos were plentiful and helpful. The artistry was amazing. My budgeted wine allowance was spent on varying shades of concealer, foundation makeup, and same-day delivery charges. Between self-loathing and a hangover, I didn't want to look at another drop of alcohol for years. I was done.

Little did I know amid my alcohol-fueled crisis, Tiffany was having one of her own. I didn't know what Tiffany was up to. Our cyber communication was nothing more than a controlled, cryptic message of what she wanted me to know. Besides, I was busy making a wreck out of my own life, pun intended.

How much damage could an eighteen-year-old cause in three months, I'd occasionally ask myself. I wouldn't accept the real fears growing in my head. It was a lot like my drinking. I was a master of inventing ways to monitor and conceal my addiction. But in my mind, heart, and soul, Tiffany was perfect. The only truly good, golden thing in my life. She couldn't be having any problems at UT. At this moment, her professors were writing letters of recommendation for fully-funded summer abroad programs and for placement in next year's honors college.

The truth, I would soon learn, was Tiffany's grades were slipping. It wasn't because she wasn't smart enough to do the work; that's rarely the reason the dropout rate for college freshmen is over fifty percent. I know statistics like that; I've spent nearly thirty years warning students of the dangers of binge drinking and taking drugs, but as far as personal application was concerned, I was pathetically blind.

Students failed because they didn't go to class. They were too busy partying and sleeping it off. Tiffany was no different. Neither was I. Get drunk, mayhem will follow.

Thanksgiving would bring Tiffany and me many things we would never be thankful for.

Chapter Five
Over the River and Through the Woods

The screech of metal-on-metal brake pads resounded inside the house. I walked out on the porch as the hatch-back Honda pulled into the driveway. The first thing I noticed after the siren call of the brakes was the huge dent right below the gas cap. It immediately killed every good intention within me, realizing the time and money it would take to fix it before Tiffany went back to Austin. A paycheck for Brake Buddy, "Your Brakes' Best Friend," jiggled in my head. Funny, I never met one affable person in that miserable repair shop.

From there, things quickly fell apart. Tiffany emerged from the Honda looking like Death itself. She had lost about ten pounds; her hair was dirty, and she was still wearing the makeup she put on the night before. The raccoon eyes of smudged mascara and smeared eyeliner always gave it away. When I hugged her at the front door, she stunk. She smelled like sour milk.

"Hi, hon. So good to see you," I said too loudly and too quickly. She knew. She knew immediately what I thought of her.

"Don't start, Karen. I'm going back to bed. I can wake myself up when I'm ready to get up. Try not to stomp your feet and bang things in the kitchen to do it for me."

She walked into the house and dropped her suitcase by the front door. She acknowledged Poncho sleeping on the couch with a rub of his spine, then slipping out of her shoes, she walked into her bedroom and slammed the door.

She slept sixteen hours. I periodically checked her breathing. I wanted to cry my eyes out when I saw her fingernails—they were stubs of red, swollen skin and ragged pieces of nail. She didn't even move when I picked up each hand to study it carefully. I placed them back underneath the covers and kissed her on the forehead. I just watched her. I stood over the bed and watched her small chest rise and fall with breathing.

I spent the day and that night Googling the warning signs of addiction and buying brown rice, beets, radishes, artichokes, cabbage, broccoli, and seaweed to detox her once she woke up. I made up my mind to force feed her if she refused to cooperate.

After that I emptied every bottle of wine, beer, and liquor I had into the kitchen sink. I boxed up the cute little wine glasses I bought and stuffed them into the attic. Out of sight; out of mind. Oh, what a simpleton I was.

She woke up at two the next afternoon. I saw her bedroom door open from where I was standing at the stove. I was making soup with all the detox veggies I bought. She walked bleary eyed to the kitchen table and slumped into the chair. I had to control every sinew in my body not to grab her and cry, "Tiffany, what happened? What happened to you, honey?"

Instead, I gave her a quiet smile.

"Get your shower. I'll have a sandwich and a bowl of soup for you when you get out."

"I don't think I have any clean clothes in my suitcase. I haven't had time to do laundry," she said, studying the patterns in the kitchen tile.

"That's all right. I'll get you a little sundress and some clean panties. It's in the eighties today. It's that global warming thing. At Christmas, we'll be opening our presents in shorts and tee shirts."

"Okay," was what she offered me and a chance to look at her, as I moved closer to her, still standing in the kitchen, staring at the tile floor. Her face was as white as a piece of notebook paper with those blue-green lines running across the surface like a million equators. Oh, I knew where she had been. I just didn't know what she had lost along the way.

"All right, girlie; get your shower and let me finish making my soup," as I dismissed her without heeding every nerve in my body that screamed hold her, hold her, before she blows away.

"Karen, I know what you're thinking, but you need to stop staring at me."

Tiffany sat directly in front of me at the table, moving the spoon back and forth across her soup bowl. She averted her eyes to the vegetable soup swirling in front of her.

"I just don't know how you could have lost so much weight in so short a time. You're like the opposite of the freshman fifteen theory. You're supposed to gain. Is the cafeteria food that bad?"

"No, no, the food isn't bad. I'm just having a tough time keeping up."

"What do you mean, keeping up? With school, with the reading?"

She let the spoon clank against the side of the bowl and looked up at me.

"I can't compete."

"What? I don't believe that. You're a smart girl, Tiffany. What are we really talking about here?"

"The girls are beautiful and smart, Karen. Not just average smart, but gifted smart. They're like the Olympian idea of perfection. Their clothes are perfect; their teeth, their hair, their cute BMWs and their rich dads and pretty moms who visit them for tailgating home games. They own the damn RVs they park at the stadium. I'm just nothing, nobody. I just can't compete. So, I got a little messed up, behind in the work, mostly, mostly because I was lonely."

"Oh Tiffany. I told you not to go to the Greek mixers. No wonder you feel out of place. There's just a falseness to that whole Greek scene. You know that. And, you know, you don't need friends like that. It's just a place to be seen. It's just a social game. A stupid game."

"I'm still nothing. Nothing with a dead dad and a mom

who hasn't spoken to me in years. What does that say about me? My own mother doesn't love me. What does that say about me?"

"What does it say about you? You? Damn it, it says your mother is worthless, not you, Tiffany."

"You see I was really okay going to high school here. I was well read and could talk about books. My aunt was the cool teacher on campus. I had an identity then, but not anymore. There's just this element there of super cool. I'm not cool."

"So you started partying to fit in? Really? How was that going to help?"

"I just needed a little something, Karen. My roommate had some Adderall. It made me feel confident in social situations. I was able to concentrate better in class."

"You're taking your roommate's prescription drugs? You're smarter than that."

"Look, Karen. It helps me with my schoolwork. That should make you happy, right? I'm going to take it. My grades are down and the semester finals are coming up. You can either take me to a doctor and let me get a script legally, or I'll take them illegally at school."

"I'm done with this conversation. I am sick to my stomach. For right now, I'm going to concentrate on getting you mentally and physically stronger before you go back to school."

"Whatever. My Adderall use is no different than you drinking wine every night. We're self-medicating, Karen. That's what people do in America. We self-medicate. Look, I just need it for a short time. Help me out, just for now. After finals, I'll quit."

"How am I going to know that? You won't return a call, much less a text."

"I'll do better. I got into a big funk and barricaded myself in the dorms the first six weeks. I'm slowly getting to know people, making some friends. You were right about the Greeks. I don't fit in. I'll stay away from the mixers."

"I want to believe you. I do. Look. Let's just enjoy tonight. Watch a movie. Cuddle on the couch with Max and Poncho. Eat popcorn. Let me think about it, at least twenty-four hours."

I pushed myself from the table, grabbing both of our bowls in one swoop. I turned around and looked at her still staring at the table top. She looked as pathetic as she sounded. It literally ripped my heart in two.

"Pick a movie, Tiff. I'm going to put some corn bread on for dressing tomorrow. We'll have our Thanksgiving meal early. Let's make it a nice one, enjoy each other and the day. I think we both need it."

"Sure," she mumbled, shuffling from the kitchen table to the couch, where she evaporated into the pillows and the cat.

I laid awake that night, staring into the darkness, searching for an answer. What was the right thing to do? Give her Adderall legally and send her back to Austin or refuse and wait for the phone call from the police, telling me she was busted? She just made it, so easy for me—put me right there between a rock and a hard place.

There were plenty of pill mill docs to get a month's supply without a problem. The problem with Tiffany was not ADHD, she was simply using the drug, so she could party and study. It was her time management plan. Take a stimulant, stay out all night, study for hours, make it through school.

I could drag her back here and make her attend community college. Try to manage her that way, but the social repercussion would be enormous. She'd feel like a loser, and when you feel like a loser for long enough, you eventually become one. Maybe it was my ego. I didn't want to tell anyone at school my kid couldn't make it through a semester at UT.

That thought alone sent me reeling with guilt. I'm just as messed up as her. With that death sentence, the tears began to fall across my face onto my neck. I was afraid. Afraid and alone. Everything was out of control. I pulled my mother's handmade quilt up to my neck and sobbed into the frayed, calico patchwork of pink, green and lavender.

Before the divorce, before the steady pounding of wine, before all the disappointments I swallowed down year after year, I had faith. I prayed. But I gave up on all that feel good, fool your-self stuff right after Mom and Dad died. That was the first test God didn't pass. My beautiful mother and father died in a ditch alongside I-10 in a drunk-driving accident. It was Christmas Eve! Christmas Eve and they were gone, and the drunk survived with a hangover. That was the Christmas before Danny died. If I'm keeping score here, it was also a few years before Sherry abandoned Tiffany. *Where were you, God?* I didn't call out to Him that night or any other night. I didn't know God anymore, and I knew He had forgotten me a long time ago.

Chapter Six
The Fall

The morning light brought the realization that Thanksgiving would be like every other day of the year, something to get through. I poured the first cup of coffee with Max and Poncho at my feet. The three of us walked out into the front yard. Max, never one to wait, bolted. Half asleep, I watched him gallop toward Leona Supak's perfect house and yard as it resonated in middle-class splendor Thanksgiving morning.

As I watched Max squat in her yard, I noticed the curtains part in her living room window. The front door opened and there was Leona. She had to be the only woman I've known in my entire life who refused to do anything about the massive amount of facial hair on her upper lip and the giant, angry brow extending across both eyes.

"Damn it, Karen. Why do you allow your huge dog to defecate in my yard every day?" Leona proclaimed at the curb.

"Happy Thanksgiving, Leona. I'll get that cleaned up right away for you."

"You don't always get it all, Karen. Just last Monday, I had to wash my tennis shoes after walking in my own front yard. I'm sick and tired of . . ."

"Let me get them back inside. I'll be right over."

Max refused to move when I called him. Repeatedly, I begged him. I finally gave in by running back into the house and grabbing two processed cheese slices wrapped in cellophane. I handed the dog his cheese, and he finally moved when I called. The three of us walked back into the house, panting against the closed door and an angry Leona. I filled Max and Poncho's bowls with food and water, and grabbed a plastic bag and a garden spade from the garage.

When I crossed the street to begin my duty, Leona gave me a look of disappointment as her one eyebrow screwed into a grey W across her forehead. She stepped back into her house and watched me from the living room window.

One drama down; twenty-three hours to go! I fortified myself with another cup of coffee and began mincing onions, celery, garlic, and raw oysters for the turkey dressing. After I rinsed the defrosted bird, I patted it dry and stuffed it.

Our Thanksgiving was miserable. I couldn't bear to sit at the table any longer than Tiffany. All the beautiful food I had prepared, green bean casserole, cornbread dressing and giblet gravy, sweet potatoes with brown sugar and butter—all the dishes she loved since childhood she simply picked through. She never once looked at me. Instead she ate with one elbow on the table, propping her head up with her other hand.

"Tiff, remember how you use to eat all the fried onions before I could put them in the casserole?"

She didn't answer me. Her eyes remained fixed on the food before her, occasionally she'd move her fork back and force across the food, moving it from one end of the plate to the other.

"I could always count on buying two cans of fried onions and two containers of Cool Whip, because you'd polish them off before Thanksgiving arrived. Funny girl. You'd curl up on the couch and eat Cool Whip like a bowl of ice cream."

I laughed out loud hoping to encourage her to join me in a conversation. It did the trick, all right.

"Karen, I'm too tired to talk." She ate a forkful of mashed potatoes, picked up her plate, and put it in the sink. She went into her room and didn't come out again.

Thanksgiving. It took me four hours to prepare the food we spent ten minutes eating. I cleaned up the kitchen and went to bed. Sticky pad note to self: eat out next year.

Chapter Seven
Band-Aid on a Bullet Wound

Breakfast began for me, Max, and Poncho at 6:15 a.m. Tiffany emerged from her room at 1:00 p.m. By then, I had enough time to do what I had to do.

The Heights neighborhood was crawling with pill mill doctors, those cash only Dr. Feel Goods who prescribed a diet pill or antidepressant for thirty days only. No refills. These docs did business with one pharmacy, ensuring the pill mill plan was a direct route, prescribe and deliver, with no middle men collecting their portion or spilling the beans.

The pill mill waiting room was a standing-room-only crowd of young adults, housewives, and middle-aged single women—those afflicted with social anxiety disorders for underachievement in the game of life. They were either too fat, too thin or too human to run with the winners without help from pharmaceuticals.

My colleague Kelly was known to frequent these places a time or two for quick weight loss prior to spring break. When I called her for a recommendation that morning, I visualized her opening a little black book and scanning the D for Docs tab with a pointed red fingernail tip.

"Holiday blues, Karen?"

"No, raising a daughter blues."

"Well, why don't you try Dr. Whitmire? He won't even charge you for a physical. It's a total of five minutes. Ask and you shall receive."

"It's just a little something to get me through a tough time."

"I'm not judging you, Karen. Look, he's only going to give you a thirty-day supply and a skewered right eye, warning you not to return."

"Thanks, Kelly. Think I can get an appointment today?"

"It's a first-come, first-serve office. Just get yourself down there and take a number. It's like fast food medical care."

"Have I really sunk this low?"

"Welcome to the twenty-first century. This is how the rest of us live."

I hung up and turned around to face Tiffany. She heard everything. Okay, I made a pact with the Devil, why try to paint it pretty.

"I'll do it. All right. I absolutely hate myself right now, but I'll do it. I'll get you Adderall for one month to get you through finals. Never again. You'd better get your act together or I'll drag you back here, and you can go to HCC with all the other kids who can't make it through their freshmen year at a state university."

"Go for the jugular, Karen."

"No, sweetheart, you went for the throat when you showed up here looking like that. You took the first swing. Now, we're in the ring together."

She yawned in my face then went back to bed. I took a shower, dressed myself, and got in the car with no makeup and wet hair. Thus, my journey began, supplying the person I loved most in the world with a drug that was not prescribed for her. I had a reason I assured myself. Neither one of us could handle the social pressure of Tiffany not performing in college. As a middle-aged, single woman, she was my only affirmation. Yep, we were sick.

I dropped the Honda off at Brake Buddy, caught the courtesy shuttle back to the house, and jumped into the Jeep. Siri would escort me to the pill mill. I wasn't alone in this mess, after all.

Dr. Whitmire's office was located on Greenway Drive, a side street nestled between used car lots and Fitzgerald's Night Club. My ex and I spent a lot of time dancing and falling in love at that place. Somehow the literary name made you feel somewhat smarter than the average club goer, although you were pounding beers and sweating to live music the same as the working man at Joe's Place.

Fitzgerald's even had an additional bar downstairs, cleverly called Zelda's. But that was a long time ago, when I loved Greg and Greg was going to be a civil rights lawyer and make the world a better place. *I was that young.*

I pulled into the parking lot Dr. Whitmire shared with PAY DAY LOANS NOW! I ran a brush through my wet hair and hid behind my sunglasses. The opened door to the office offered metal folding chairs, a room full of screaming kids, and women scanning their cell phones. In each corner of the room stood plastic palm trees coated in grey dust. On the floor were assorted puzzle pieces and a twenty-year collection of *National Geographic*.

The closed frosted reception window suddenly slid open and a troll with smeared mascara under her eyes spit out, "Sign in on the clipboard. Cash or insurance? You file your own."

"Cash," I quipped and signed the clipboard with the pen attached with tape, twine, and staples.

I played with my cell phone for two-and-a-half hours, before the door leading to the wonders of modern medicine finally opened.

"Karen Anders."

I stood up and followed a young Asian woman in a lab coat and bright pink rubber shoes.

She weighed me, took my blood pressure, and recorded the numbers that have betrayed me my entire life on a laptop in a small white room. She looked at me, twisted the straight black silk of her hair into a ponytail, then secured it with the pen in her hand in an impromptu bun. It created the illusion of a suspended black waterfall slightly above her head.

"Dr. Whitmire will be in shortly."

I nodded at the waterfall above her head and the door closed. I wondered if I should get undressed and lie on the examination table. No way. I sat in the plastic chair next to it and played with my phone.

Dr. Feel Good finally appeared. He was white, short and sported a nasty little goatee on his chin. The second thing I noticed about him was the picante sauce stain circling the second button of his lab coat.

God, help me. Why am I here?

"What can we do for you, Ms. Anders?" he asked, scanning the laptop on the counter.

"I've had a hard time concentrating at work, Doc. I'm sure it's just early menopause. But I've got my annual review coming up, with a lot of documentation due. I'm wondering if you could give me something just to get me through the month. That's all I have to do. Get through my annual review at work. One month should help me."

He never turned around and looked at me, as he typed away on the laptop at the counter. He pulled a prescription pad from his lab coat pocket and began writing. He handed me the slip of paper reading, Adderall 20 mg, twice a day. No refills. At the bottom of the paper, his name was stamped.

I started to make a little joke about rubber stamp medical care, but I stopped myself.

"Fill that at Optimal Health Pharmacy; it's two blocks south, then a left. Good luck with your annual review, Ms. Anders." He looked at me for the first time, then he left, leaving the door open behind him. I took my twenty-first century certificate for successful living and placed it in my purse.

Chapter Eight
Up and Down and All Around

Tiffany was prepared for her return to Austin with a one-month supply of Adderall and Tupperware containers of organic soups and casseroles. The food was a mad woman's approach to combating any hint of drug addiction with the illusion of homemade goodness. I thought of what my ex would have said, "The road to Hell is paved with good intentions." He was a notorious "told you so." But I ignored the premonition as I placed a huge bottle of Vitamin C in the bag for good measure.

I was an optimist when it came to Tiffany as I stood in the driveway, staring at her. She was preparing for her drive out of here, away from me, away from self-control. I chose to believe she would change her attitude, her grades, and her hair color by Christmas.

"I know. The Dr. Pepper color doesn't do much for my complexion."

I nodded and smiled.

The approaching New Year promised a new girl. I believed her, because I had to. She smiled at me, backed out the driveway and didn't look in the rearview mirror. The tiny voice deep within began whispering to me as I watched the dented Honda move down the street. *Just the beginning. Just the beginning. Just the beginning.*

The repetitive refrain was a reminder we were robbing Peter to pay Paul. The Adderall would provide jet propulsion during the day, but the night would come with the body's demand for sleep. How would she sleep? How would she come down from the amphetamine? The cheap, easy depressant alcohol would arrive. And like a dog chasing his tail, becoming more frantic in his delusion, Tiffany would spin deeper into the hole she dug for herself until the hole became so large, she couldn't crawl her way out.

I stood in the driveway with Max and Poncho for a while longer. We stared at the spot where Tiffany had been only a few minutes ago; then, we stared at Leona's house across the street. I imagined she and her eyebrow were staring back at us.

"Come on Max, let's go eat some turkey and dressing. Poncho, can of tuna for you." I coaxed the animals back inside.

Anxious and hungry, I filled the emptiness inside with a microwaved plate of green bean casserole, turkey, dressing and gravy. After four glasses of Syrah and a full belly, I turned on some Christmas music and took the Thanksgiving decorations off the porch. Inspired by the Australian full-bodied red, I danced my way into the attic and lugged down the artificial Christmas tree conveniently stored in a giant sock. Drunk and OCD, the night had just begun!

"Jingle Bell Rock" boomed in the background as I unfurled the artificial branches of the Scotch pine in front of the living room window.

"This year, Leona, I'm going all out. There'll be lights on anything standing outside, and the sound of Christmas music coming from a speaker on the porch," I announced to the open living room window and hoisted my wine glass as a sign of neighborly cheer in her direction.

When I stepped backward from the window, my foot got trapped in the string of mini-pumpkin lights I took off the porch earlier, and I fell into the coffee table, careening with a ceramic Santa. Its pieces lay on the floor near me.

"Stupid drunk," I announced to the staring dog and cat. I left the merging of the two holidays in a broken, unorganized array in the living room, turned out the light, and sprawled across the couch, staring into the darkness.

I found my cell phone in my pocket and sent Tiffany a text. "I miss you already."

Max found a spot on the couch near my feet, while Poncho settled into the chair next to us. "I'll Be Home for Christmas" floated above the iPod and swirled above us. Sad, lyrical, sweet, I sang the familiar words, "If only in my dreams."

My cell phone rang somewhere between the couch cushions.

"Got your lesson plans done yet?"

"Hey, Kelly. No lesson plans, but I visited your Dr. Feel Good." Max eyed me and jumped to the floor.

"Well, how'd it go?"

"I did it. I willingly participated in an illegal act."

"Welcome to the dark side," she laughed.

"You made it look too easy, Kelly. You've got me drinking in bars and breaking the law."

"Are you calling me a bad influence or a fun person?"

"Neither. I guess I'm really living now instead of hiding in my job and responsibilities."

"You're normal, Karen. Don't be so dramatic. Hey, let's plan something fun for Christmas break this year, instead of catching up on grading and cleaning the house."

"Let me get through today, Kelly. Then we can talk hedonism for the middle-aged."

"Sure. Hey, I got bus duty in the morning, so you won't see me for coffee in the teacher's lounge."

"Too bad. I'll catch you during first lunch."

I hung up the phone, kicked the decorations, and made my way to the kitchen table. I sat at my laptop and pounded out my lessons plans.

> *English III—Emily Dickinson and the themes of isolation in poetry. Student will demonstrate the ability to interpret literary elements in "The Loneliness One Dare Not Sound" by writing a free verse poem on the same theme.*

English IV—Gulliver's Travels. Literary analysis in-class discussion. Literary Essay, 3.5. Student will demonstrate the ability to write a literary essay, using a thesis statement based on the novel's central theme of physical power or moral righteousness as a governing factor in social life.

What this jargon meant was I would pound my head against the chalkboard for hours. All the students would remember is how weird Emily Dickinson was and the names of the little people who tied up Gulliver. I hit send and off the lesson plans went into cyber storage of the best intended plans.

I drank three large glasses of tap water, dismissed the thought of carcinogens in Houston's water supply, and turned out the light in the kitchen.

A quick shower and I was in bed with Max at my feet and Poncho on my head. I reached over to plug my cell phone in and saw a red number one on the message app. My heart leaped.

"Thanks 4 everything. ♥"

My Tiffany. My girl. I calmed myself before I replied with a parade of dancing emoticons. She'd hate that. Keep it simple. Steady.

"Work hard. See u in 3 weeks for Xmas. ☺"

I'm allowed to use emoticons too! The secret is not using too many. Besides, the smiley face softened the work hard statement. I closed my eyes and prayed, something drunks and liars are compelled to do after a long weekend.

Help me, God. Help me know the real reason for Christmas this year. Let it flood my heart. Bring it into this house. Watch over Tiffany. Help her despite my poor decisions.

Chapter Nine
A Noble Profession

The life raft theory came into play three weeks before Christmas break. People see an end to their struggles once land is in sight. With that, they lose rationale for surviving the final leg of the journey. For my English IV students, this meant a lot of bad attitudes.

"How do you know Jonathan Swift was talking about greed when he met the Yahoos? The Yahoos? Come on," questioned Jason Novak, a smart aleck fullback on the school's varsity team with a one-way ticket to Texas A&M, a six-figure sales job, and Sunday golf at the country club.

"That's why we study literature, Jason. Swift's work is political satire."

"Why are we even talking about something that happened that long ago? It's no longer relevant."

"Well, someday when you go to a cocktail party you'll have something interesting to add to the conversation."

Deadly silence. I broke my number one rule: don't get on the same level as the students and expect to win an argument. The use of the word relevant is what got me. *Smart aleck.* My feet were expanding from my shoes in an angry red mass. I needed to sit down and shut up.

"Mizzzz Anders, I'll just slit my throat right now, if that's my future."

Every nerve in me wanted to reply, "Here, let me help you with that." But, instead, I offered a smile and an announcement.

"Class, I want a 3.5 essay with a solid thesis statement on the central theme in *Gulliver's Travels*. I'll write it on the board for you."

I did a quick spin to the board that left me dizzy. I wrote, "*Gulliver's Travels*: central theme of physical power or moral righteousness as a governing factor in social life."

I turned back around to face their bewildered faces, holding on to the podium to stop my spinning. "It's due at the end of class. It's worth twenty percent of the semester grade."

I know. Cheap shot. I wasn't out to win teacher of the year. I was out to survive the next hour. Oh, the joy of watching thirty-two seniors toiling away in silence. I had a tug of guilt thinking most of them couldn't read on a twelfth-grade level. I'd come up with a remedy later when averaging grades. Well, at least they were still listening to me, as I watched their heads bow over sheets of notebook paper. They believed my threat, except Novak.

"What does that mean?" he asked, pointing to the chalkboard.

"We've just discussed it, Jason. You'll figure it out." With that, I sat down at my desk and kicked my shoes off. Instant relief.

Five minutes before the bell rang, I offered a bone.

"If you're not finished, it's homework. Turn it in first thing tomorrow."

Thursday rolled around before I knew it. I had survived another work week with wine, cable television, and online shopping. The weather offered a reprise for the holiday season by swinging a limp eighty-four degrees with hundred percent humidity to a chipper seventy-one degrees. The nutty Algebra teacher down the hall began wearing her seasonal cat sweaters. Oh, the joys of the trite holiday rituals, but it did improve my mood. I wanted a happy Christmas, but I didn't feel lucky enough to get one. But I could dream of one, and my dreams were of seeing Tiffany sipping hot chocolate, sitting at the foot of the Christmas tree.

My phone gave a pleasant buzz on the kitchen table while I was grading papers and eating dinner Thursday night.

"2 more wks."

"I feel it 2. Can't wait."

"Met someone."

"Oh?"

"He's really cool."

My brain searched the many definitions of cool. Cool as in noncompliant? Cool like drugs, sex, and rock-n-roll? Laid back cool Snoopy? I instantly got a happy visual of Tiffany and a normal-looking guy holding hands and smiling. Puff, it was gone. I couldn't get that lucky with Tiffany's choice in men. I had four years of high school dating hell to remind me of that.

"Nice guy?"

"Met him through gaming site."

"Gaming site?"

"Face-to-face this weekend."

"Hope it's a busy, public mtg. place."

"U worry too much."

"Call me afterwards."

"Say good night, Karen."

"Night-night."

I did a quick online search of gaming. Of course, I'm the last person on the planet to know this has been going on for years! It's a virtual world of 3-D chatting for people who don't have the social skills to ask someone out or they don't care about ever getting out. I had a sick vision of her slumped over a computer screen into the wee hours, as her mind and body tried to dispel the speed effects of Adderall.

I'd like one normal day in today's world. One normal day. Whatever happened to a guy liking a girl, asking her out, and getting a pizza? No need to date, just game. Where had I heard of this before? Gaming marathon? One of the teachers was talking about gaming weekends for the high schoolers. They set up their computers in hotel rooms and play nonstop, eating endless bags of potato chips and drinking canned energy drinks. They don't stop to sleep, gaming twenty-four hours throughout the weekend. Forget personal hygiene. That went out the door with normalcy.

I finished grading papers and drinking a bottle of wine. I

topped the night off with a sleeping pill and a glass of Houston tap water. Sticky note to self: stock up on vitamins, wine, and aspirin for the weekend. *Ah, the unholy trinity of the middle-aged.*

"Happy Friday, girl," Kelly proclaimed from the coffee station in the teacher's lounge. I walked closer to get a better look at the tee shirt she was wearing. Casual Fridays usually meant another opportunity for Kelly to rage against Kenny Ramsey's inane dress code.

The black tee shirt had large white lettering underneath a picture of Neil Young reading KEEP ROCKING IN THE FREE WORLD. She wore a multi-colored cotton full skirt with purple tights and red Chuck Taylor high tops.

"Is this another fashion statement aimed at Kenny?" I asked.

"There's nothing wrong with self-expression, Karen. At least here in Houston, we can still dress the way we want to without being arrested."

"We're a city state here at Heights Central. Kenny is the emperor. He's going to keep hounding you. Is this just a test of wills?"

Kelly laughed and pushed a stray curl into the bun on her head held in place with two hot pink chopsticks.

"I realize it's petty, Karen, but I'm between men, bored in my career, and forced to dye my hair every three weeks to hide the grey. Let me have some fun for God's sake. Yes, it's juvenile, but I've been down in the trenches for so long, that's my mentality. It's Friday, and I'm celebrating with this little costume I'm wearing."

I checked for notices and phone messages in my box while she smoothed the wrinkles from her skirt with the back of her hand.

"No news is good news," I said, finding only a flyer for the HCHS Honor Society's bake sale at lunch. "Hey, I'll see you tonight at Fergal's, right?"

"Yeah, where else would I be on a Friday evening?"

"All right Debbie Downer, try to have a good day. See you tonight."

The first block bell rang, and I pushed myself into the throng of teenagers moving through the halls like cattle to the slaughter—confused, stunned, and dangerously powerful in a group. I made it to my class a minute before the tardy bell and unlocked the door. In they came. My first block class always reeked of pot and cigarettes. Then there were the "What am I doing in a place like this?" students who greeted me each morning with a look of disgust and quickly resigned themselves to the desk I assigned to them on the first day of the school year.

"Happy Friday, young scholars. Today we discuss Samuel Johnson and the first dictionary of the English language."

At the end of that declarative sentence, half the heads in the room fell onto their desks. Some with a pronounced thump. Ten minutes into the hour, I had to keep the game up.

"Yes, young nobles, Samuel Johnson, poet, literary critic, and philosopher, received the most recognition for his dictionary, but he was also known for some quotable quotes. In your assigned reading, did you find a favorite?"

There was a stir in the back of the room; behind a giant purple backpack, a small voice rose. It was Joel Perez. He hadn't said a word the entire school year, except "here" whenever I called his name while taking roll.

"When making your choices in life, do not neglect to live."

"Joel? Did you say that? It's hard to hear you from where I'm standing."

"Yeah, I like that quote."

"Tell me again, Joel. I want to write it on the board."

It pained him to have to repeat himself, but he did. In large capital letters, I wrote on the board in front of the class: WHEN MAKING YOUR CHOICES IN LIFE, DO NOT NEGLECT TO LIVE.

"Thank you, Joel. Courtney, what do you think Mr. Johnson meant by this?"

By now, a third of the class was staring at the words on the board. Courtney was paralyzed in her desk.

"What does he mean by choice, choices in life?" I encouraged.

"Well, like if you're gonna be a hipster, a jock, a druggie, or a freak. Like doing what others want you to do. Are you really living your life or are you living through others' ideas of who you should be?"

All eyes were on Courtney. And me, well, I was in teacher heaven. I wanted to grab Courtney, hug her, and let her know she was brilliant, but I couldn't. I couldn't embarrass her. Instead, I quickly diverted my attention to the rest of the class.

"Exactly, Courtney. Hey, let's all think about this quote on the board. Here's the buy-in on this assignment. There's a twenty-five-point bonus on the semester final in two weeks. Tell me what you think about the quote. You've got to use a thesis statement, then back it up with at least four complete sentences. Think about it. I want five or six great sentences."

The first head down with pencil in hand was Joel Perez. I watched his bowed head of thick, wavy blue-black hair and somewhere in me a prayer escaped. A prayer that life would give him beautiful things to read and think about. *It's what separates us from the village idiots, Joel. Run from them! Have the courage to be you!* Surprisingly, a little tear escaped from my eye, and I felt very good about being Karen Anders and the choice I made years ago to be a high school English teacher.

Before class ended, the overhead speaker came on. Voila! Our principal, my pal Kenny, reminded us the yearbook would begin taking individual pictures in the gym. I had completely forgotten. I searched my desk for a note, maybe an email on my laptop. Found it.

"Hey that's us, guys. Seniors are always first with pictures. Get your backpacks and purses. We won't come back here. I'll do another roll call in the gym, in case you're thinking of skipping out. Okay. Everybody out. I'm locking the door behind me."

The poor girls sat together on the bleachers in the gym, waiting for their individual names to be called. They sat in groups. Hispanic girls. White girls. Black girls. Segregated by skin color, integrated by poverty.

Lakesha Williams stood up when the photographer called her name. Instead of walking toward the camera, she faced the girls in her group. Beonca removed the silver-toned bangles around her wrist and handed them to Lakesha. Erika put her index finger into her mouth, lubricating the rhinestone ring stuck on her finger with saliva.

"Girrrl, you sick," laughed Lakesha, taking the offered ring from Erika, wiping it against her jeans to remove any remaining saliva before placing it on her own finger.

The last offering was from Tela. She removed three nylon scarves, black, silver, and gold with black tassels, and put them around Lakesha's neck. Lakesha grabbed a tube of purple lipstick out of her jean pocket and pushed it across her lips. Pouting, she faced the photographer. He directed her to the stool in front of the camera. And like magic, the same magic I witnessed year after year on picture day in a public school, the camera's image portrayed the girl differently. Lakesha Williams became a pretty girl, not a poor girl.

Friday at dusk I gathered with the other beasts in the Houston jungle at the watering hole known as Fergal's Pub. The bar flies, that sad little group of guys and gals who succumbed to making Fergal's their home, buzzed around the bartender. The only difference between me and the swarm was my matchy-matchy outfit with chunky costume jewelry. *So obvious.* I had one foot slowly sliding into their world and one wobbling in the respectability of my day job. But loneliness is a hateful companion, gnawing the soul into the late hours of emptiness. I could do a day job until I dropped dead in the classroom. It gave me a purpose, a schedule, a place to be. But after that, filling those hours in an empty house, I was lost, lost in the Merlot.

"Buy you a drink, sailor?"

"Hey, Kelly, you just rescued me from myself." I gave her a little hug and looked down at the blue jean cut-offs she was wearing with black tights and Chinese Coolie slippers.

"I guess the first one is on you for doing the duty."

I ordered two draft beers at the bar and carried them to our usual table in the back.

"Two more weeks and then the break. I can hardly wait," Kelly clunked her mug against mine.

"Then what do we do? Spend the time off taking down the Christmas decorations and grading papers?"

"Actually, I was going to mention this later, but now's the time. I think you can use it. After your mystery visit to the pill mill and your bad attitude since Thanksgiving, let's plan a little road trip."

"Depends on where the road is going."

"My sister and her family spend Christmas through New Year's in Crested Butte, skiing and acting like they own Colorado. I can offer to watch her dogs while she's gone, and we get the big house on Barton Creek on the redneck Riviera."

"What does that actually mean?"

"We can eat her food, drink her liquor, and take Uber into Sixth Street and hear some live music. We escape the Houston malaise after Christmas."

"Okay. Why not? I'm sure Tiffany will blow me off after Christmas Day."

"Look. You've got to create a life for yourself, Karen. It's time. You've been a great parent to her; now she's moving into the next stage in her life. You should too. You'll still be her parent, but not so hands-on. It's a natural process, leaving home and becoming an adult."

"What do I do with Poncho and Max while I'm in Austin with you?"

"We'll take them, but that cat has got to be in a carrier. I'm not driving to Austin with a cat on my head."

"Poncho will be in a carrier. He prefers it when traveling. You're right. Let's have some fun and stop worrying for a while."

Carl found us in the back of Fergal's.

"Aren't the wings fifty cents tonight? Where's our wings, ladies?"

The alarm sounded at 6:00 a.m. on Monday morning. Poncho, Max, and I started the week with hope.

Chapter Ten
How Low Can You Go?

On Friday at 1:16 p.m., the last day of school before the Christmas break, I received her text. I was on cafeteria duty with just a few minutes to go before the bell rang and the last class of the day started.

"Can't come home for Xmas."

Just like that, Christmas was over. The gifts, the cooking, the movies, done . . . the shopping . . . done. Over and out. Loud and clear. I waited a good twenty minutes before I responded. I was too busy picking up the pieces of my heart that had just been twisted out of my chest.

"Why?" I texted. Simple and direct. Who could dodge that bullet?

"Can't make it on allowance. Had to get a job."

Now my heart wasn't just broken, I was mad. I could have run to Austin on the adrenaline pumping through my body. I stood against the lime green wall of the school cafeteria, watching teenagers make a huge mess of their food, dropping it on the floor between conversations and yelling at the person at the table across the room. I closed my eyes to the madness of these two worlds colliding: work and the evaporation of a personal life. I replied to Tiffany's last text without going into the cave with her.

"No problem. Coming to Austin for New Year's with a friend. See you then."

No, that wasn't how I felt. I wanted to know why her plans

had changed, but I couldn't take the risk of being hurt by the truth. It's hard to accept that your kid doesn't want to see you. But not coming home for Christmas was beyond mother-daughter angst or generational divide. It was unusual, weird, the stuff that happens to other people, never you. After all, I gave this kid everything I had to give. I loved her until it ached. And, it wasn't enough. I was in that whispery, lower-voiced caste of shameful mothers other mothers talked about. Me.

I couldn't handle that truth coming out of her, so my text to her was nonchalant, cool, easy-breezy, no problem, whatever, Tiffany. I'll just celebrate Christmas with a dog, cat, and gallons of cheap wine.

I looked away from my cell phone just as a milk carton stuffed with mashed potatoes and green beans exploded on the back of an unsuspecting freshman. I didn't know the kid's name, but I knew millions like him over the years of dusting off and up-righting underweight, pimply nobodies everyone hated. I looked down at my phone before walking towards him.

"K." And that's all she wrote, folks. I sighed and declared underneath my breath, *I HATE MY LIFE*, then smiled weakly at the freshman groping for lumps of potato on his back with both hands.

"Need some help?"

He didn't answer me but looked into my eyes, giving me that same look I have seen a million times. The look that resonated, I HATE MY LIFE. We had something in common.

"Do you know who did this?"

Again, that look and no answer.

"Give me a name and you don't have to deal with this anymore. No one will know what you said to me. That kid will be gone. It's really the only way to stop this."

I reached out to touch his shoulder as a sign of trust. He immediately backed away from me.

"Just leave me alone, lady."

"Okay. Let me at least get you a hall pass for an extra ten minutes to get to the bathroom and clean yourself up before the next class."

I scribbled on the pad, signed it, and gave him another smile of encouragement.

The same look. No answer.

I walked away, determined to find Kenny Ramsey. He had to do something about the bullying. It was out of control, especially in the halls between class and at lunch. There just weren't enough teachers on duty during the lunches to watch for everything. Of course, I was on my phone during duty. I wonder if anyone saw me texting.

I saw Kenny with the four football coaches and the three basketball coaches in front of the soft-serve ice cream station. Huddled, yes, huddled together in a little circle. I immediately thought, a gathering of apes in the jungle.

"Hey, Kenny." I didn't mean for my voice to come out nearly that loud or accusatory, but it did. The eight apes looked up from their conversation as I clicked my sensible pumps toward them. I might have had my hands on my hips. I don't know. It all happened quickly.

"Karen?"

"There's not enough teachers on lunch duty. There was another incident of bullying. I don't know who threw the food across the room, but it hit a freshman in the back. It's humiliating for the poor kids who continue to be victimized during lunch. You've got to get more teachers out here to help."

"Karen, seven men are on duty now. If you include me, that's eight. We didn't hear or see anything."

"Really?"

"Yes, really. By the way, I didn't see you on duty. Where were you standing?"

"By the green wall the whole time."

"That's not a designated area for lunch duty. Why did you stand there?"

Here we go. Now, I'm the bad guy. Can't I just get out of the building today before anything else happens?

"Right, well, I just forgot. Last day of school before break, trying to juggle too much."

All eyes were on me. I was waiting for him to deliver the last punch.

"Karen, I won't write you up this time, but no more favors. If my memory serves me, you're supposed to be standing near the fresh fruit station."

"Yes, you're right. I just forgot." Then suddenly the balloon cartoon of a gathering of apes wearing coaches' shorts and nylon shirts appeared in my head and out it came. "If I were where I was supposed to be, I could have offered you gentlemen some bananas. You know we just can't get enough potassium, especially at our age."

I didn't wait for a response. I spun on my sensible pumps and stomped away from any rebuttals.

A pathetic, two for $2 microwaveable meal and a low, sinking feeling slowly spread across my psyche Friday evening as I stared at the TV, occasionally running my finger across the plate of orange sauce left from the Oriental Chicken DeLite I had just devoured. Poncho sat judging me from the overstuffed chair in the corner. Max couldn't care less what mood overtook me. He was happy just to have me sitting by him. I loved that dog, the only living creature on the planet that loved me unconditionally. Poncho didn't care if I dropped dead tonight, as long as his food bowl was filled before I kicked over.

Eleven more days to go until New Year's Eve. How, how was I supposed to do this? What would I do about Christmas? I don't think I have ever been alone for Christmas. Sticky note to self: take a cruise next year.

I stood up and stared out the front window across the street. Leona's porch light was on. It was always on, day and night. How many years have Leona and her eyebrow done Christmas alone? Well, that explains it. Spend a lot of time alone and you end up hating dogs and letting your eyebrows merge. You just simply give up on living and join the existing.

I poured myself another glass of Merlot and considered the profoundness of the living versus the existing. I didn't want to be in the other camp. I needed a plan. Draining the glass of wine, I walked to the bathroom and took two sleeping pills from the cabinet. I guess that was the best plan I could come up. I'd simply make a better plan tomorrow. *After all, tomorrow is another day, Scarlett.*

I woke up Saturday morning in a complete fog from the sleep aids. I grabbed my robe and felt something sticky and moist. It was last night's Oriental Chicken DeLite orange sauce. *Forget it. It's too early to be fashion conscious.*

I opened the front door for Poncho and Max. I saw her immediately in a pastel-striped snap front duster, reaching for *The Houston Chronicle* in her well-trimmed yard. As she looked up at my slamming of the front door, Max took off, ran across the street, and lifted his leg against her perfectly appointed Shepherd's Hook and its adjoining planter swinging with angel-wing begonias.

"Karen, KAREN, why do you refuse to control your animals?"

I couldn't face the humiliation of her seeing the orange sauce stain on my robe, so I whistled for Max, coaxing him home. I edged a bit closer, but far enough, so she couldn't see the stain.

"Sorry about that, Leona."

"You always say that. You just don't care. You don't respect other people's things." Leona's eyebrow rose into her forehead with each word she volleyed from across the street.

"Come on, Leona. That's not true. I appreciate how nice your yard always looks. It's the best one in the neighborhood."

Here she comes. She's crossing the street.

Then suddenly she was a few inches from me and I saw the complete Leona Supak, the dark circles, the pursed lips, the lined forehead and the one, huge, angry eyebrow stretched across it.

"Young lady, I've lived across the street from you for years, for years, and now, I know. Now, I understand. You don't control your animals; you don't respect your neighbors, because, because, just look at you. You're still a young woman and you've let yourself go. When was the last time you washed that robe?"

Ouch. Was it the hangover or the brain fog from the sleeping pills that made her words vibrate painfully in my head? I didn't know what to say. She hurt me. Damnit, Leona hurt my feelings. So, I picked up my worthless cat and cried on the curb in front of my yard with Leona and her eyebrow staring me down.

"Oh, for Heaven's sake, you're not crying, are you?" Leona demanded.

"You're mean, Leona. You're mean to my pets and me. What did I ever do to you? What? I try to wave and smile at you and your perfect yard every morning, every evening. How dare you call me a mess. As if, as if, I didn't know I was."

"Come here. Come with me, Karen."

With that simple command, she took my hand. Poncho and Max obediently followed behind as we crossed the street and entered her kitchen. She escorted me to a 1970s dinette, stuck a homemade cinnamon roll in front of me with a cup of black coffee resting on a white saucer. She placed a spoon on a paper napkin, next to a sugar bowl and matching creamer filled with milk.

She sat directly across from me, patiently waiting for me to begin my story. I didn't feel like talking, so I cried, ate the cinnamon roll, drank the coffee, blew my nose in the tissue she handed me, then asked for another cinnamon roll.

She filled up the coffee cup and put another cinnamon roll in front of me. I cried with gratitude. Then I cried some more while eating the second cinnamon roll.

"You're going to have to come up for air sooner or later," she smiled at me.

I laughed.

"Leona, do you want to be friends?"

"Yes, Karen. I think that would be nice."

"Okay. I need a friend. Well, I think I need a mother. I'm sorry. That's too much to put out there."

"Look. Do you think you're the only one coping with loneliness? It's a world full of lonely, disappointed people. The entire human race is constipated with loneliness."

"Well, I never really thought of it that way. You're right. I know it. But I'm going home. I'm embarrassed by my tears, this disgusting robe . . . everything." I stood up to leave.

"Here. I can see how long it's been since someone made you something to eat, just to be nice."

"Oh God . . ." Sobbing, I took the plate of cinnamon rolls with me. Max and Poncho followed in single file. I was almost to the front door when she called my name. I turned around.

"Karen, come over Christmas Eve at seven. I'll make us a nice ham."

"I'll bring dessert and . . . wine." There I said it; it was out in case she didn't realize I was a drunk simply by my appearance this morning.

She waved back at me as I pushed the front door open with my right hip. In the safety of my own home, I collapsed on the couch with Poncho on my head and Max at my feet. I could hear it. Faint at first, then louder. The rock-solid fact I could not hide from, no matter how much I drank or carried on with the neighbors. I am alone and I've got to do something about it. I'll see Leona for Christmas Eve. I'll fill eleven days until I can see Tiffany. I'll be okay.

Chapter Eleven
The Ghost of Christmas Past

I knew it was him. The stance, the sandy-blond hair that slightly curled at the nape of his neck. That BIG BUTT of his that immediately reminded me how lazy he was and probably still is.

It's Greg. I know it's him and he's with his wife. Barbara, Barbie, Babette. I look horrible and I'm holding a twenty-pound bag of cat food in the fifteen-items-or-less aisle, like some pathetic middle-aged, single woman. Help me, God. Please don't let them see me. Look at her. Beautiful. Slim. Blonde.

"Karen, Karen, is that you?"

Busted. Should I ignore the call? Maybe they'll think it's someone who looks just like me and go on about their business.

"Hey, Karen."

I turned slightly. It was not a full body shot, but a slight turn to the right, slimming my body with the large black metal display of candy bars, mints, and chewing gum. It's an instant ten-pound eraser.

"Is that you, Greg? Oh, my gosh, it is. And? So sorry, I've forgotten your name."

"Barbara, it's Barbara." It was just like him to answer for her.

"Right. Well, I'm picking up some last-minute things. Headed to Crested Butte to do some skiing for Christmas."

He knew I was lying the minute I said it.

"Nice. How's Tiff?"

Of course, he would say her name like that. Half a name like she was half a person. *It's my pet name for her, not yours!*

"Great. At UT. I'll pick her up in Austin and we'll fly from there."

"Nice. Well, Merry Christmas." With that, he tried to peer over the magazine and candy counter to get a full view of me. *Don't stop the damn checkout line, Greg. This is the flagship grocery store, the Texas-owned HEB located at the elite intersection of San Felipe and Fountainview. It's chock full of the rich, richer, richest, who never talk above a whisper or place sixteen items in the fifteen-items-or-less line.*

Greg stopped and turned to nod at Barbara, Barbie, Babette. She flashed a polished veneer smile and off they went.

I paid for my items and walked slowly toward the double glass doors ensuring enough time for Ken and Barbie to ooze out of the parking lot in something black, European, and expensive, before I could be seen in full view. I spotted my car instantly. It's always amazed me how my mind opened and closed like a vault when I needed it to. Thank God, I was spared the humiliation of wandering the lot carrying a twenty-pound bag of cat food. I got in, slid the safety belt across me, and looked in the rearview mirror. I wasn't surprised by what I saw. I was nothing but a big fat liar in pajama pants with pet food slumped in the passenger seat next to me. The lowest of the low. I'm sure they didn't believe my lie about skiing in Colorado over the Christmas break. I might just as well have said I'm flying to the Moon, join me. That was the life I wanted, millions of light-years away from the life I lived.

That evening I sat down at the kitchen table with an empty red and white container of Egg Foo Young and Leona's perfectly white porcelain dish, finger-swiped clean of cinnamon roll crumbs. I took a blank stationary card with a cheery pasture of bluebonnets on the front and wrote my neighbor of eighteen years a thank you card. Eighteen years across the street from Leona and we never once shared a meal or a cup of coffee until yesterday. Was that a reflection of my pathetically routine life of work, home and grocery store or another casualty of social media? How strange to post information online to a world of strangers and not even know your neighbor beyond the oddity of a female with one giant eyebrow.

It wasn't even Lent and there I was feeling the need to love my neighbor as myself. Actually, I should love her better than myself.

I washed the plate and taped the note to it. Combing my hair with my fingers, I proceeded across the street without Max and Poncho. Her porch light was still on. She answered the door after the second knock.

"Hi, Leona. I wanted to thank you for your kindness the other day."

"Well, Karen, how nice to see you again. Feeling better?"

I looked that old woman straight in the eyes and lied. "Yes, I'm afraid you caught me during a hormonal surge."

"Oh?"

"I loved the cinnamon rolls." I pushed the plate toward her with the note taped to it.

"What's this?"

"Just a little thank you note. I'm looking forward to our Christmas Eve."

Before she could open it, I called out "Thanks again" and spun back toward my side of the street.

I didn't even turn around to wave goodbye. I gave her my backside with one hand waving goodbye in the air, calling out for all to hear, "See ya Christmas Eve."

I locked the front door behind me and fell on the couch with Poncho purring at my feet. I gave him a lazy massage with my heel.

"Let's give Tiffany a call. Not a text, mind you, but a call," I announced to Poncho and Max.

She answered and my heart began to flutter.

"Hey, little girl. How's the working world?"

"You wouldn't believe the number of people wanting a veggie burger and a tattoo before Christmas?"

"What?" Despite myself, I laughed out loud.

"It's crazy, but hey, I make good tips."

"I'm coming for New Year's. I've got to see this place, maybe

I'll do the combo, too. I'll take a rose tattoo on the buttock and an alfalfa and avocado sandwich to go."

"Come in New Year's Eve. I'm working, but I get double holiday pay. Jared's the manager."

"Jared?"

"Yes, Jared, my boyfriend."

"Oh, well, did you get his name tattooed on your chest, 'cause it's the official employer ID or are you in love?"

"You're still good at the one liners, Karen. You'll meet him. He's nice. You should act nice, too."

"Is this the same guy you met online, gaming?"

"Yes, Karen. He's also the manager of the Ink & Juice."

"Ink & Juice? What the hell is that?"

"It's where I work. Where you're going to visit me and where you're going to eat the best whole grain veggie burger you've ever had in your life."

A sense of dread filled me from the back of the skin crawling on my neck to my toes, so I changed the subject. At least we were communicating. I had to find some comfort in that.

"What do you want for Christmas, honey?"

"Just you, a nice meal, and a day-off."

"That's too easy."

"How about an old-school Christmas? Maybe some really comfy jammies, a robe, and giant, fuzzy slippers. I think the trio should match, don't you?"

"I can hardly wait to get to the store. Are you still a pink girl?"

"I am! Hey, got to go. Customer up! Love you. Bye."

The phone went dead in my hands, but my heart. My heart! That amazing organ was pumping in my chest, about to fall out. I was filled with hope. Sweet Tiffany. She was that same girl. Maybe she was over the Adderall binging. She sounded so normal.

It suddenly felt like Christmas. Goodwill toward man, love and charity, and all those things that keep us going despite the reality of life. I wanted to go to church; better yet, I wanted to be on my knees praying. Before the feeling left me, I grabbed my purse, backed the Jeep out of the driveway without glancing back, and steered it towards St. Thérèse Catholic Church on Haskell. That's where I was married, once upon a time, when I believed a man and a woman could mate for life. I was a different girl then.

Behind the rectory was a small parking lot with the Adoration Chapel to the right. A rose garden with a marble statue of the Virgin Mary separated the two buildings. My mother and the other women of the altar society planted that rose garden in 1971. The world was very different then, too.

When I opened the door, the immense silence and peace of the chapel engulfed me as I made the sign of the cross, then quickly made my way to a hidden corner of the little room, away from the windows, the entrance door, and any do-gooder Catholics.

I lowered my body to the worn, faded red carpet of the kneeler in front of the monstrance and heard the words of my childhood, the Jesus I use to know.

Abide in me, and I in you.

Do you still abide in me, Jesus? Do you know the woman I've become, a drunk, lonely and afraid of everything around me?

I couldn't pray, but I could cry. I cried for every hurt Greg and I hurled at each other; I cried for my sweet mother and father; I cried for every broken kid who ever sat in my classroom; I cried for my Tiffany, out there in this crazy world, winging it. I cried for every morning I woke up to an empty wine bottle and glass next to my bed. I cried until I was exhausted, lying down on the pew with my eyes closed. I slept the sleep of the emotionally purged, numb and empty.

"You are loved." A voice whispered in my ear, placing a warm hand on my head.

I didn't want to open my eyes. I wanted to stay there on the pew with the whispering voice and the hand on my head, as if I were a child, a little girl in the luxury of carefree sleep, that underworld never disturbed with regrets and anxiety.

But with reality seeping in through my tightly closed eyes, and the sounds of the world outside the chapel window, I bolted upright, rotated my head once to stop the pain in my neck and looked the do-gooder straight in the eyes. A tiny Mexican woman about seventy years old with a large wooden Rosary in her left hand was sitting next to me on the pew.

"Are you okay?"

"No, I'm not all right, but that doesn't make a difference in the large scheme of things, does it?"

"Excuse me, I just thought you might need some encouragement. You looked so abandoned there."

"Oh," squeezed out of me. Then I began to cry again. She moved closer to me on the pew and patted my bowed head.

"You are not alone," I heard her whisper next to me, and she began to smooth the hair on the top of my head.

"I am alone."

"No, you are my sister in Christ."

"Jesus doesn't know my name."

"Yes, he does, Karen. He is sitting and crying with you, now. Lay down. Rest. Rest with Him."

I laid my head against the wooden pew and closed my eyes. When I woke up, it was dark outside the chapel windows. The tiny Mexican woman with the wooden Rosary beads was gone.

Chapter Twelve
Peace on Earth, Goodwill to Men and Dogs

I woke up Christmas Eve morning with a clear head and a plan. Despite the fact I had to go to Wally World, 212,000 square feet of chemicals, plastic, and food all under one roof, I was determined to stick with the plan.

I felt almost optimistic, strangely energized. Was it the encounter with the Hispanic woman in the Adoration Chapel or dinner with Leona that night? I was also a short week away from seeing Tiffany. I had a lot to look forward to this Christmas season. A few weeks ago, I was devastated with the prospect of facing the holidays alone. It all changed from crappy to happy in a few days. I can do this. I can follow a simple plan. Be thankful. Be sober.

I picked up three gorgeous, gold-foiled wrapped poinsettias at Wally World and drove to the Memorial Gardens Cemetery off Eldridge Parkway. By the number of cars in the parking lot, I realized I wasn't the only one missing those I loved at Christmas. Grief barreled up to the asphalt parking lot in different sizes—double cabbed pick-up trucks, shiny European SUVs, and gas-hugging compacts. My little Jeep squeezed in between a solid white Land Rover and a dented Kia. I always thought the most economically diverse place in America is a cemetery. You may get a cheap seat in the very back without a shade tree, but there's a spot for you. Death, the great equalizer, takes us regardless of wealth, fame or zip code. For the living, we get the daily reminder of how it could have been, if only. . . . There wasn't a day that passed, when I was not haunted by the unkept promises and unspoken words I should have given my parents and my brother.

I always remembered where to find Danny, Mom and Dad. The guideposts were a cement bench opposite St. Michael the Archangel. It was always the same initial reaction, despite how many times I'd been, through all the years, through every season, in every kind of weather imaginable, *why?*

I sat down on the bench and placed the three poinsettias next to me. I was numb with raw emotion, despite the fifteen years passing since I buried my brother. I simply never got used to the fact my family was gone.

It was a typically warm day in December, even by Houston standards. My flip flops and sleeveless dress made it bearable. The sky above was clear with a few Cumulus clouds, cotton-ball puffy, assail in the blue. They moved slowly in the south wind. I thought of Wordsworth. I thought of all the years trying to press upon the teenage mind the relevance of a nineteenth-century English poet.

I first learned the poem in my high school English class. That was many years ago when boys gave girls ID bracelets as a token of love, and English teachers made their students memorize poetry. When I try to explain that time to my students today, they're bewildered. If I define that time as before AIDS or herpes, they are in shock.

I whispered the first lines of the poem like a little prayer for that time long ago, for that girl I was long ago.

> I wandered lonely as a cloud
> That floats on high o'er vales and hills,
> When all at once I saw a crowd,
> A host, of golden daffodils;

Alone in the cemetery, I repeated the poem at least three times, thinking of each word as part of a chant to the clouds, the deep green of the grass, and the red of the poinsettias at my feet. I knew loneliness well, but I had learned, like Wordsworth, to find a tonic in the natural world.

I knew my students understood loneliness. It was written on

their faces. Broken families, fickle friends, cruel first loves—they knew loneliness better than a middle-aged adult who survives by simply turning the heart off and self-medicating, numbing what is regrettably lost in our youth.

Loneliness as a tangible emotion was never lost on teenagers; that's why they loved Edgar Allan Poe. Poe went for the jugular in the madness and cruelty of loneliness. My students never did understand the comfort in nature, no matter how many times I beat the idea of Pantheism and the Romantic poets into them. Teenagers were savvy enough to understand their parents' flower power generation, but they were years away from comprehending the soulfulness of a flower.

I sat on the cement bench until an unleashed chocolate Lab bolted toward me, breaking the silence of the morning. The meditative mood was gone forever trying to figure out why someone would bring a dog to a cemetery. The dog was happy enough, but not everybody is a dog lover. *It's not a private cemetery, folks; you've got to think of other people.*

I saw the owner, a young woman, running toward me and the dog. Despite myself, I petted the dog. He smiled at me. Yes, the dog smiled at me. I could see it in his eyes. He was loving me and loving this moment, tilting his head to the side, so I could scratch that little spot right behind the left ear. Ecstasy oozed from his low moan and half-closed eyes.

"Hey, sorry about that. He has a mind of his own when it comes to open spaces."

"Oh, it's okay; I'm a dog person. We all sort of speak the same language, don't we?" I smiled at the young brunette with a pixie haircut and smart brown eyes. She could have been one of my students from a few years ago, wearing an Astros tee shirt and blue jean cut-offs with flip flops.

"Well, Merry Christmas. I know being in a cemetery the day before Christmas can be a sad way to begin the holiday. I hope yours is good."

I smiled at the woman and her dog. They were a couple. They had each other. But I couldn't help wondering who she was visiting in the cemetery. Who was the brunette with the smart brown eyes grieving for this Christmas, last Christmas, and every Christmas, forever?

I sat on the bench for a while and watched them walk away. Did the girl come to pay respect to a mother? A father? A brother? Or maybe she was like me. She'd come to cry for all three.

Well, I didn't come to sit; I came to pray. I walked toward the grave sites and placed a hand on my mother's tombstone and I prayed for them, my sweet mother, father, and brother I missed so much. I prayed for the woman I was all those years ago when I spent a Christmas Eve recovering from a telephone call that would change me forever. Mom and Dad both gone Christmas Eve. Now, there's a Christmas present you can drink to.

I wouldn't allow myself to think about what this Christmas would be if they were still here. The food. The gifts. The belonging to something other than myself. It was too much, too much loss. I wouldn't torture myself with it.

I placed the poinsettias on their graves and stepped back, allowing my mind to take it all in. Too much. Too much for anyone. I could either give in to a one-woman pity party or leave. I decided to leave. I said another prayer and walked away, repeating their names over and over in my mind. *Mama. Daddy. Danny. Mama. Daddy. Danny. Mama. Daddy. Danny. Mama . . .*

Marching back to the car, I got my energy level up. I had too much to do to drown myself in the past. I thought about tonight's dinner party with Leona. Should I even attempt to go to Christmas Mass beforehand? Should I invite Leona to go? I think she's of some Slavic descent; she'd have to be with those eyebrows and the oddly managed facial hair above her pursed lips. Who was Leona Supak? I started the car and stared at myself in the rearview mirror. Crow's feet and all, I was completely exhausted with the possibilities and decisions of the day and it wasn't even noon.

Chapter Thirteen
The Eighty-Year-Old Orphan

I was ready for Christmas Eve dinner with Leona at 5:00 p.m. With two hours to kill, I applied my lipstick three times, pressed the wrinkles in my red and green tartan skirt with sweaty palms, and scanned her yard for unusual activity from my living room window. An hour before dinner, I began accessorizing my holiday costume. For fun, I pinned a shiny metal Rudolph with a blinking nose to my collar. *Is this even fashionable anymore? Well, maybe in nursing homes in the Midwest and Bunco groups in the South.*

I didn't want to start drinking before I got over there. My nerves reminded me every second within every ticking minute. I bought a nice German Riesling to go with Leona's ham. For dessert, an overpriced cheesecake from French Kiss Bakery sat on the kitchen counter, along with a gold foiled wrapped poinsettia. Christmas Eve with Leona—what would the evening bring?

At six straight-up, I called Tiffany. She answered on the third ring.

"Merry Christmas, baby."

"Hey, Karen. I miss you. Doesn't quite feel like Christmas in the tattoo parlor."

"I guess not," I laughed.

"It'll be good to see you. Can't wait for you to meet my boyfriend."

"I'll bring your presents with me. What should I pick up for your man? Does he read?"

"Yes, he reads. What kind of question is that?"

"Oh, you know, what types of books does he like?"

"Apocalyptic zombie stuff."

Well, for once, I didn't have a pithy little retort, because I was immediately filled with hate for this clown.

"I'll hit River Oaks Bookstore before I come. Take care of yourself, honey. I love you a bunch."

"Wait a minute. We can talk some more. There's no one here. I'm done with my menial tasks for the day. Work is work. It can wait, especially since I have to do a shift on Christmas night."

I wasn't going to comment on the grotesqueness of a combo tattoo parlor and vegan restaurant being open on Christmas. Really? How pagan can you get?

"Karen . . . you still there? What's up for Christmas?"

"I'm having dinner tonight with Leona. Probably have a few drinks tomorrow with Kelly and Carl, exchange our gag gifts. Same thing we do every year."

"Who's Leona?"

"Good Lord, Tiffany. She's lived across the street from us your entire life."

"Oh, the old lady with the eyebrows."

"We've become neighborly since you've moved. She's quite the cook. Her cinnamon rolls are to die for."

"Glad you're making more friends, Karen. You deserve to have some fun."

Was this Tiffany I was talking to?

"Yes, my little world is getting bigger every day."

"Hey, got to run. Customer up and the payroll clock is ticking. Oh, forgot to tell you. The car needs a water pump, at least that's what Jared thinks. Anyway, I'm dependent on others for transportation until the next paycheck. Call you later. Merry Christmas."

"That Jared is just a Renaissance man with all those job skills."

"Stop. I just told you Merry Christmas and you have to ruin it by judging my boyfriend"

"Okay. Sorry. You know I often talk before thinking. Don't hold my sarcasm against me. It's just a bad habit."

"Say goodbye, Karen, before we start fighting."

"Bye, baby. See you soon. Love you."

The phone went dead. Sticky note to self: research Apocalyptic Zombie Fiction as a legitimate genre in literature.

I reminded myself to curb the sarcasm with Leona. Turning off the kitchen light, I grabbed the wine, cheesecake, and poinsettias and headed across the street. The neighborhood was aglow in mini white lights, and for the die-hard camps whose red and green HUGE bulbs still powered up, a little tint of merriment haloed their front porches. Leona fell into that camp. She probably had the original box they came in. There was comfort in a simple cardboard box with a cellophane front, providing the buyer a peak at the product. One single red Christmas bell and one single green Christmas tree gave a visual interpretation of when to use the product. I loved the simplicity of it all. My parents swore by the GEM Christmas lights they purchased when I was born. I can still hear my mother's declarative sentence, "Best $1.75 I ever spent."

I stood underneath the red and green glow of Leona's front porch for a few minutes before knocking. I was on a sentimental journey in a world that no longer existed.

Leona opened the door before I could knock.

"Merry Christmas," I proclaimed and thrust the cheesecake, wine, and poinsettias forward.

"Merry Christmas," she replied, effortlessly balancing the three items, while eyeing the tartan skirt and the metal reindeer pinned to my chest. She was wearing a white, lacy blouse with smart black pants and even smarter, low-heeled black leather shoes. She wore a rope of pearls around her neck and smelled of Chanel.

I knew Leona was no South Texas girl among many in the swamp of Houston. She was European. I could tell by the slight accent, possibly eastern European, and her fondness for an orderly yard and gourmet pastries. The pastry queens of my childhood were my paternal German grandmother and my maternal Czech grandmother, who made fruit kolaches and cheese rolls—light, fluffy little jewels, never over-sugared but just the perfect blend of fruit, butter, and cheese. My grandmothers' birthday cakes for me were jewelry boxes of eggs, flour, and milk with powdered sugar and cream cheese frosting. But, that was a long, long time ago.

No one made birthday cakes anymore, once the celebration grew into a competition among mothers and children. Forget pin-the-tail on the donkey, usher in the stretched limousine with a dangling mirrored ball for the third graders. Who needed a home-made birthday cake when you could have twenty cupcakes flown from The Cupcake House in Manhattan for the second graders? Recalling a homemade birthday cake soon merged with "When I was a little girl, after walking twenty miles in the snow and ice to go to school . . ." No one wanted to hear it; no one cared.

I snapped to attention under Leona's gaze at the door, fell in line across the threshold, and gave up any false pretense of what the night would offer. I was going to have fun with this woman. I parked myself in a cozy wing-back chair near the artificial Christmas tree and sighed out loud. It's amazing how comfortable you can become once you let go of the death grip of control.

"Let me get us a glass of wine, Karen, and I'll join you."

"That would be lovely, Leona." I smiled at the alliteration in my reply. Always the English teacher, but I didn't want to start being a smart aleck after the first glass hit me. *Better keep a lid on the sarcasm, Karen.*

"Riesling. That's an interesting choice."

"Yes, well, I thought with the ham. Hope you like German white."

"I do. It's so warm tonight. Who ever thought Christmas Eve with forty percent humidity and seventy-two degrees? Chilled white will be refreshing."

I did a quick scan of the living room. Every stick of furniture had a doily on it. Crystal, doilies, and an 11x14 print of Jesus pointing at his bleeding heart above the fireplace screamed eastern European. There were no other pictures in the living room. No candid shots of grandchildren on Grannie's lap, no 1982 freeze frame of a bride and a groom in a bad tux with large lapels, and no family reunion portrait from a long-ago Thanksgiving gathering. *Did Leona belong to anybody?*

"Here you are." Leona extended a bejeweled hand and a golden iridescent goblet toward me.

I took it immediately to my lips. The golden warmth filled my entire being with a sense of calm. *Steady girl, steady; don't gulp it down like a desperate drunk.*

"How nice. Thank you." I smiled at her as she sat across from me on the extremely flowery sofa with extremely flowery pillows to match.

"You look much better than last time I saw you," Leona said, eyeing me carefully. I decided to put down the wine glass as if it were a very casual thing to do, as if it didn't matter to me what was in the glass. Casual. Light. No pressure here. Clutching it in my sweaty palms was a dead giveaway.

"Oh, you know, I was just missing Tiffany. Then there's the hormones."

"I don't see her car much. I suppose she has gone on with her life."

That went straight to the jugular. And with that note, I grabbed the wine glass and drew slowly, purposely from it.

"Young people. That's what they do. They grow up and move on with their lives."

Oh, for God's sake, did she mean for that to be a huge statement on the human condition?

"That Tiffany, she just loves being a college girl, even working her way through to help pay for the tuition and books. How's your family, Leona?" Yes, it was a cheap shot; it was cruel to say that to an old woman with obviously no family, but I needed to set some boundaries before taking another glass of wine. Leona was not ruining my buzz.

"I don't have a family. There was Albert and me. That's it. I said goodbye to what was left of my family when I left Germany after the war. Married an American GI. Not so out of the ordinary in those days. I was a waitress in a cafe in Bavaria, near Fürstenfeldbruck Air Base. The GIs came in and out of there. Imagine, the entire town was no more than GIs, coffee and cigarettes. I couldn't believe someone had enough money they could just light it on fire and puff it away. But the Americans did. After work, I'd pick up the cigarettes they spit out of their mouths onto the ground. Money to throw away! I'd take my little collection home, remove the unsmoked tobacco and reroll them in fresh paper. I'd sell those soldiers the very cigarettes they threw away. Ha. The absurdity of making money after a war. The Germans got the Deutsche Mark, and I got a husband, all in 1948."

She got up from the couch, smoothed her white blouse and walked into the kitchen. *Should I follow her in there?* I finished the rest of my wine, listening to her bang pots and pans in the kitchen. Fortified, I approached the kitchen.

"Karen, set the table. Use the china in the cabinet. The silverware and linens are in the cabinet drawers."

Yes, ma'am.

I sat down at the opposite end of the table when I finished setting the table. A few minutes later, Leona began an assembly line pace of placing covered casserole dishes, mashed potatoes with gravy, English peas, Brussel sprouts, yeast rolls, and a large baked ham on the table between our two chairs. After the fruit salad was served individually, she gave me a long direct look and walked back into the kitchen. When she returned, her lipstick was fresh and her apron was gone.

"Let's have a blessing of the food," she announced, making the sign of the cross rapidly, then bowing her head she whispered, "Bless us, O Lord, and these Thy gifts, which we are about to receive from Thy bounty through Christ Our Lord, Amen."

"Amen. This looks great, Leona. Thank you so much."

"It is a small meal. More wine?"

"Yes, thank you." The old woman got up and served me again without a smile. My remark to her earlier in the evening continued to burn.

"I'm sorry if I hurt you, Leona with what I said earlier. I can be very direct at times. I can be terribly sarcastic, yes, even rude at times. Forgive me. You opened your home to me on Christmas Eve. Here's a toast to your health and peace in the coming New Year."

She raised her glass to me. This time it was I who walked to her side of the table to touch her wine glass with mine.

"Merry Christmas, Karen. I should have had you and your daughter over many years ago, but today is a new beginning for many different reasons."

"Yes, to new beginnings." Our glasses clinked again, and I walked back to my chair.

"Now, help yourself."

I loaded my Bavarian china plate, encircled with gold ribbons and light green and pale pink cherry blossoms, with mashed potatoes, peas, and two pieces of honey-glazed ham.

"Did you buy your china in Germany, Leona? It's beautiful."

"It was a wedding gift from my husband. I think the day I got it was also the day I ate my first piece of fruit. I believe it was an orange. There wasn't much food during the war or immediately after."

"Yes, I am sure the war, with all its rations . . ."

She put down her fork and knife and looked at me.

"Rations? People were starving. Rations were the first years of the war."

She took a long draw from her wine glass.

"Oh. I didn't mean, well, I don't know much about post WWII Germany, Leona. I certainly didn't mean to belittle the situation."

"No one knows much, except the people who were there. I was just a young girl, Karen, who happened to make it to the western side of Germany, where the Americans were. I walked, at times traveling by boat, the 500 kilometers to Passau in Bavaria, traveling at night, following the Danube, fear and hunger, knots in my stomach, eating tree bark and potatoes this big."

She raised her smallest finger, indicating the size of potatoes being half of her raised finger.

"I would go to the fields and dig at night, searching for anything the farmers had left behind during the day. All I wanted to do was get to where the Americans were. Away from the Russians. I saw what they did in Budapest."

I picked up my plate and wine glass and sat next to her. I

looked her in the eyes and placed my hand on her right hand, resting on the tablecloth next to me.

"Tell me about your life, Leona. I'm sure you've figured out how small mine is from watching me across the street. But I want to know your story. I think we were meant to be friends."

She sighed heavily, and with that I let her take my heart and soul with her as she traveled in time seventy years to Budapest, Hungary, where she stood on the banks of the Danube, a ten-year-old-girl, searching for a sign from God in the hills of Buda.

Chapter Fourteen
The Brief Beautiful Life of a Happy Little Girl

"My maiden name was Molnar. I came from a good Catholic family. My father was a butcher working in the best market in Pest, making sausages, the best cuts of beef, pork, lamb, and chicken. My family had the best spices in all of Hungary. You could smell the paprika and onions mixed in the pork sausages blocks before you arrived at the red and yellow door of the shop. Next to it, an old woman had a bakery, Mrs. Bala. She and her daughters, Luca and Fanni, made Dobos cakes, fried langos, dumplings, tarts . . . the best in the city!

"Ahhh, that was my childhood before the war. God, family, and food—that is what we lived for. Walking with my mother and father to Mass at Matthias Church, in front of the Fisherman's Bastion in the foothills of Buda. That was our Sunday. Beautiful mother and father. My Apa and Anya. Patrik, an older brother, died in infancy. I was an only child very much adored by my parents.

"My father had a great shock of black hair that spilled over his forehead. He was always pushing it aside, showing his large brown eyes beneath fierce black eyebrows. Mother was fair, a blonde. A slender woman who dressed neatly. No dirt beneath her nails. No mud on her shoes. She was a lady, a lady without a title. My parents were very much in love as a couple. Oh, I know now how lucky I was to have them. You know, Karen, not every child is born to a couple who are in love. It is a rarity. Beautiful life for me, a happy little girl. Gone. Gone." Leona's voice trailed into silence. I smiled at her and patted the top of her folded hands on the table.

"Yes, my story, now, now, yes, I remember quite a bit even at my age. My mother worked for the Hapsburgs, as her mother and grandmother had. They were quite good to her. Generous people. I often wore the clothes of their children, handed down to me. Smart, little dresses and smocks, hand embroidered from the finest seamstresses in Hungary.

"The Hapsburgs' son, Otto was a bit older than me; he lavished me with gifts of fruits and candies. He'd make a little present in his personal handkerchief, wrapping fruit or candy inside, then tying it into a knot. He'd give that little present to my mother before she left her position each day. Without fail, Otto did that for me every day until the war scattered us from each other.

"We were a people strangled between Hitler and the fascist coward, Szalasi. What chance did we have! Szalasi fled early on; a true monster that man was. Christmas Day 1944 delivered Stalin. Yes, like you Americans say, it was the nail in the coffin. That was a day I would no longer be a carefree little girl holding the hands of my mother and father as we walked through our beautiful city on the Danube.

"Clear and cold that morning was. My mother and I walked along the riverfront, looking for food, perhaps some carp along the Pest side of the Danube. We had been in the central market earlier, looking for food. There was none to be had. So, we thought we might be lucky to trade my mother's bracelet, the last of her modest collection of jewelry, for a small piece of fish along the riverfront.

"It was dangerous then, as it had been since the war started. The Danube was easy transport for contraband, soldiers, and murderers. It was especially good for refugees with money and papers to leave the misery far behind. But today the river front was pulsating through the cobblestones we walked upon, fear, fear, fear with each step. People were crowded together, shouting, 'The Russians stopped the trains. They've come to kill us. Hurry. Hurry. They will destroy us all.'

"My mother and father couldn't believe it, but that was exactly what they planned to do, just like the Mongols before them. For fifty days the Russian army raped, burned, stabbed, shot, and starved 38,000 human beings. Grandparents, mothers, fathers, children. Civilians. The beautiful city of the Danube, the jewel of the East, became a living hell.

"It was that very day, Christmas Day, the fascist group, the monsters known as the Arrow Cross Terror lined Jews on the east bank of the river. At gunpoint, they forced them to remove their shoes and empty their pockets. They shot them. All of them. Their bodies fell backwards into the river and floated on the current. What remained on the water's edge . . . their shoes, their shoes. Their shoes were more valuable than their lives.

"Everything, everything began to fall apart shortly after that. My parents would search for food in the city at night. It was too dangerous to be seen outdoors during the day. Our lives were a routine marked by the search for food at night and hiding from the Russians during the day. Most mornings I would wake to find them sitting at the kitchen table. If they found food the night before, a piece of bread or potato would be on a plate for me. I never saw them eat. Never.

"One morning I found myself alone. No mother and father. No cheerful little plate in front of my chair with a piece of bread. My parents were either murdered or taken to a camp. They simply disappeared from this very earth. Never, never to be seen again. I was alone in the house, waiting, waiting for days for them. I prayed beyond all hope they would simply walk through the door, awaken me, and we'd sit at the little table again.

"I did not light a candle nor leave my bed the entire time they were gone. When my parents were gone the first few hours, I waited at the kitchen table for them. But as the hours passed into night and another day, I hid in my bed. I was too afraid someone would see me at the kitchen table and know I was alone. I could have been taken. In those days, children were not spared. No one, nothing was spared.

"Alone. Alone for days, months it seemed to me, just a little girl who knew she would never see her mother and father again. Perhaps it was the third day or so that I went to my neighbors. They were a young family with children to feed and care for, but they took me in.

"We never left the house once the Russians took the city. The real horrors occurred. True horrors. An orgy of violence, mass rapes and the kidnapping of girls, yes, just little girls, who were taken to Soviet officer quarters, imprisoned and raped until they were executed. Those with the audacity to survive were deported to forced labor camps in Russia. Hundreds of thousands, imagine, hundreds of thousands, murdered."

Leona said nothing else for a long time. I had stopped eating much earlier in the conversation. Everything in the room, in the house, in the universe, waited for Leona to take a deep breath, exhaling the memories of her childhood. But she didn't. She rose from the dining room table, picked up the Rosenthal platter with the ham on it, and walked into the kitchen. I picked up the bowl of mashed potatoes and the gravy boat and followed her in there.

"Leona," I walked toward her where she stood at the stove, her back to me. She didn't turn around.

"I'm sorry for your pain. I'm sorry for the terrible loss." I placed a hand on her shoulder to ease her toward me for a hug, but she wouldn't turn around.

"It is late, Karen. I can get the dishes myself. Good night."

I froze. Nothing in my life had prepared me for this evening. Nothing in all the years of teaching abandoned, neglected children gave me the words to comfort her at that moment. *God give me the words. Help me.*

"Let me get you a glass of wine and let's sit by the Christmas tree in the living room. It's Christmas, Leona."

She turned around and faced me.

"Ah, the naïve American girl-woman. Something shiny and glittery will take away the heartache. Heartache, rejection. That's life, Karen. But you? You want more, like most women of your generation. Family, marriages, children, something to toss around, like a throw pillow on the sofa, redecorating your life, buying the right thing will give you the right life. What you've never learned is sometimes we don't get more. It is a world ruled by monsters. And when you are not looking, those monsters will come. They will throw you and your family into a river, simply because they can. Shoes become more valuable than life. Don't be so naïve to think you always get a second chance in this life."

Who could respond to that? I was guilty on all accounts, simply because I was never a refugee, an immigrant, a soldier's mother, or an abandoned child. My childhood was an echo of the American Dream, seamless, plentiful, and arrogantly happy. It allowed me to become a middle-aged adolescent, who viewed the world through sitcoms, shopping malls, and celebrity worship. Girl-woman . . .

"Good night, Leona. Thank you for dinner."

I left her house, returning to mine, quickly unlocking the door to relieve Max and Poncho. They ran into the yard, chasing each other. I stared at the house across the street, following the silhouette of Leona Molnar Supak, as she moved from room to room, straightening, cleaning, picking up, putting down; a restless ghost in a mausoleum of lace doilies, crystal vases, and the bleeding heart of Jesus.

Chapter Fifteen
Tidings of Comfort and Joy

Christmas morning. Oh, what joy! Dirty Santa, Carl, and Kelly awaited me! I took a brief look at Leona's place across the street. No sign of life. Just an existence illuminated by the turning on and turning off of the front porch light, the perpetual routine marking the beginning and end of a twenty-four-hour passing. It was the methodical X across her life's calendar.

I had nothing to say about last night. I didn't even know if I had been insulted or simply dismissed for my lack of maturity. Leona was a mystery to solve in the new year. For now, I deserved to be a full-fledged American girl-woman.

I sipped my first cup of coffee with my feet on the coffee table, staring at the television as images of mirth, joy, and families rolled through channel after channel. I had a family out there. A family of one, my Tiffany.

I didn't give her time to say anything. I offered, "Feliz Navidad, Feliz Navidad" when she answered on the third ring.

"Merry Christmas, Karen. When will you be here?"

"On the 30th or 31st. I wish it were today."

"Remember to come to the Ink & Juice, first thing. I'm working a lot before school picks up again."

"Of course, I will. I'm bringing lots of gifts, even something for Jared."

"Oh Karen, you don't have to. Just come. I need to see you and be with you."

My eyes filled with tears. "Me, too, honey. Me, too."

"Got to go. We're having his mom over for Christmas lunch."

"Oh, really. How nice. What about the father?"

"Jared doesn't have a father."

"Come on. Is the guy dead or are they divorced?"

"Jared's never met his dad and his mom doesn't talk about the past."

"Okay. Well, that certainly makes room for a million assumptions."

"Why Karen? It doesn't bother him; why should it bother you?"

She was right. I changed the subject. "Hey, see you in a few days. Merry Christmas. Love you."

"Love you, too."

Dressing for success was not the criteria for my annual Christmas Day event as a lucky charm member. I chose my usual Christmas uniform of sweater featuring a fat cat, dead center, wearing a red-and-white striped Santa cap, and a pair of black leggings to hold everything in. Black flats and the Christmas pin I wore to Leona's completed the look. Red lipstick made it personal.

I never called to find out what time I was supposed to be there. I grabbed the phone as I opened the front door for Max.

"What time are we gathering?"

"Merry Christmas to you too, Karen."

"Cut it out, you secular fool. Don't even pretend."

"Just wanted to know if you were paying attention. But come on, once an altar girl, always an altar girl. I loved my little white sheet and humble rope belt encircling my tiny girl waist."

"Ever ask yourself why?"

"Huh?"

"Why did you love being an altar server?"

"Here we go. A philosophical religious question Christmas day with an English teacher. I'm going to lose, so why even try."

"I really want to know. I'm curious."

"Well, it was a feeling. Just this incredible feeling of the entire world being outside the church doors and we were all together, praying, singing, and taking Communion. I was just a little girl, maybe eight years old, and I mattered. My small part mattered to the big picture. I felt happy and very, very special."

"I know. I used to feel that too. Happy and special, then life hit me with a two-by-four between the eyes."

"Well, come get your Jesus on at my house. I'm making all your favorites."

"What? I don't believe it!"

"Turkey, dressing, green bean casserole with the super expensive fried onions on top, broccoli with American processed cheese sauce, and a pecan pie. All for you, starting at 1:00 p.m."

"Love you, Kelly. You just made the day perfect." With a satisfying click of the phone, I stopped Max before he loped over to Leona's. We weren't in the house for three minutes when my phone rang. It was her. Leona.

"Merry Christmas, Karen."

"Merry Christmas, Leona."

"I have something for you. I hope you will enjoy it. May I bring it over?"

"Leona, I didn't get you anything."

"That doesn't matter. I will come now."

"Okay." Well, how could I say no? She didn't give me the chance.

The doorbell rang, and there she was in a wool suit of emerald green. Wool in this weather? Tradition. No matter what the cost.

I didn't hug her but opened the door for her to come in, offering a seat on the couch. Max and Poncho recognized her and immediately hung back behind the TV.

"I made Beigli; it's a traditional Hungarian dessert for Christmas. Because of my rudeness last night, you missed the beautiful cheesecake you brought over. We'll enjoy that another time." She set the aluminum foiled-covered platter on the coffee table and lifted a corner, revealing pastry rolls stuffed with poppy seed filling.

"They're beautiful. Thank you so much. Will you have one with me? I'll put on a fresh pot of coffee."

"I shouldn't. You look dressed for a party." She looked me up and down with a scrutinizing eye. *How could I compete with a wool suit and ropes of pearl?*

"I'm going to a very informal lunch with some work colleagues. Join me."

"How horrible for the host, a last-minute guest!"

"No, Leona, this woman's entire life is spur of the moment. I'll call her and tell her to add another plate to the table."

"That is very kind of you, Karen." She followed me into the kitchen and sat at the table while I made a pot of coffee.

Leona gave Poncho the evil eye as he walked the gang plank from the kitchen countertops to the small island next to the table. The look of disgust was not missed by Poncho or me, as he gave an indignant meow and jumped from the island, running into the living room.

She removed the aluminum foil for the pastries and placed the Rosenthal platter in the center of the table.

"Here, let me grab some bread plates. Do we need a fork?"

"That would be up to you, Karen."

"Okay, forks, napkins, and plates." All I could think of was the clean-up. I've lived my entire life without the formality of napkins and utensils, and I was still breathing.

"Here's a fresh cup, Leona. Help yourself to sugar and milk." I placed the plastic milk jug next to her coffee cup on the table. "I'll text my friend we'll be coming together."

I am sure Leona's blood pressure went up slightly with that uncouth touch. I sat down and helped myself to the pastry. Lovely, lovely, lovey! Each bite filled my mouth with rich poppy seeds, slightly sweet and crunchy.

"Karen, forgive me, I am uncomfortable with the luncheon plans. I am barely more than a stranger to you."

"Leona, let's fast forward to fun. I don't want you to be alone on Christmas day. I just want to be your friend, that's all. You'll laugh today. I can't promise that my friends are socially-graced, but they are bright and funny. Let's just do it."

"If you insist. Will I need to change?"

"No. You'll be a good role model for how an adult is supposed to dress."

Typical of me, I didn't think this through until Leona and I roared into Kelly's driveway. *Please God, don't let Kelly wear some leopard print get-up for Christmas day. Don't pick your teeth or your nose at the table, Carl. One normal day, people. That's all I'm asking for the sake of an old woman.*

Kelly and Carl treated Leona like their long-lost mother, and Leona loved it! The food, the passing of bowls and platters, the clinking of wine glasses and the chuckling of polite conversation made for an easy transition from last night's disaster. Kelly exhibited a Southern gentility I had never seen in her. The highlight of the meal was her standing up from the head of the table and toasting all of us.

"Merry Christmas, dear friends. Dessert, coffee, and brandy will be served on the patio out back."

She even wore normal clothes. No screaming political slogans marching across her breast in a too-tight tee shirt; no leopard print; no stilettos with fishnet stockings; no Doc Martens with army-fatigue printed shorts. Kelly looked like a nice middle-aged woman serving a Christmas meal at her suburban home dining table—a capped-sleeve plaid dress, black tights and a pair of black flats projected an All-American hostess on Christmas Day.

Our little group moved to the patio in the backyard shaded by an enormous live oak tree. We sat at the black wrought iron table with matching chairs. Kelly joined us with a large tray containing plates, forks, coffee, brandy snifters, and a bottle of Napoleon Brandy. I was happy to know she'd finally embraced adulthood by giving up on the mini red Solo cups as shot glasses.

She saw me eyeing the bottle. "A Christmas gift from an admirer," she said, smiling at me. Like a luxurious feline, confident in the allure of mystery and unattainability, the woman had many lives that no one actually knew about.

I watched Carl and Leona across from me as Kelly filled our

glasses with brandy and sliced the pecan pie. The wine and trypto-phan in the turkey lowered our voices as they became our spirits, meandering around the table, through the oak tree branches, and finally released into the late December sky of Houston. It was a dreamland of a mellow seventy-five degrees, of bold green flora and fauna.

"I've always wanted to visit Budapest, Leona. I heard it's af-fordable and the local vineyards are excellent."

"Carl, it is a beautiful country. But I still see Budapest through the eyes of a young girl, long before the war and com-munism. I returned only once, after the Russians left in the early Nineties. It was so poor. Still the wonderful food and hospitality, but the overcast of war and occupation left a permanent pale to the buildings, and yes, even to the people."

Carl, Kelly, and I held on to every word she spoke, as if we were watching a fragile flower slowing opening its petals, cau-tiously, shyly, to bloom. I placed my hand on hers, clasped into a prayer position on the table top. I hated she would repeat her sad story; I hated to see her relive such pain, but perhaps it helped her. I've spent many years of my life at the makeshift confessional of a kitchen table and a bottle of booze. Leona was no exception. She was human, like the rest of us. She smiled at each of us before be-ginning her story, luring us into her world, a world scorched from the very earth.

"My husband Albert Supak and I met in Germany after the war. He was good to me. He took me home to Budapest when the Soviet Bloc lifted. I never cared to go back since that time. Albert died just a few years ago of cancer. He suffered a great deal with the disease."

"How did you get to Germany from Budapest as a refugee?" Carl asked.

She sighed heavily, took a deep drink from the brandy snif-ter, looked out into the yard, as if searching for a place to begin. It came to her, through the silent lushness of the oak leaves, a time when she was a little girl, many years ago, sitting alone in her mother's kitchen.

"My mother went to look for my father one night after the Russians came. He had gone out before her to search for food in the city. She did not come home. He did not come home. I waited. I waited until the windows grew dark, sitting at the kitchen table with a piece of bread in front of me. I later went to my bed and waited. I don't know how long. The facts, the facts, what is a fact really with all this madness to remember? The morning came then another night. Many mornings and many nights. My mother never came back. My father never came back. Never.

"One morning I knocked on my neighbors' doors, Mr. and Mrs. Belkos. They were a young family, young mother and father, with a baby and a toddler. I had watched the children many times for Aliz and Jabir. They took me in that day, sharing what little food they could." She finished her brandy, moving the glass away from her, and looked into the yard again.

"Every man, woman, and child knows the Danube. It is a road of water, the same transport as a cobbled road like the Vaci utca, running through the city centre to Vorosmarty Square and the Grand Central Market. Hungarians are not afraid of water. It is life for us. Food, transportation, a means to bring our goods in and out through the villages and cities of Europe.

"Aliz and Jabir made a boat, a simple boat from the last of the furniture in their home and the home of my parents. I tended to the children, when I was not running between the houses, scavenging what I could from the abandoned house to the one of the living.

"Jabir studied the clouds and the wind to find the best night for leaving. That night came. It was cloudy without stars or a moon. While Jabir held the boat steady near the shore break, we each took turns climbing in. First, I helped load the children. The current of the great, black river ran through my legs like a thousand snakes as I handed baby Andras to his father. Jabir placed the baby in a basket inside the boat, covering him with a wool shawl. Next, Aliz took her son's hand, and she and Karoly laid next to each other near the basket holding the baby. I then stepped into the boat, lying next to Karoly. Jabir pushed the little boat a bit further out into the water, until it engulfed his thighs, then he pulled one leg, then another, and we became five refugees without a country, without documents floating in the Danube.

"We traveled the Danube to Passau, Germany, through Austria and Linz, praying we would not be found, traveling at night with Jabir dragging the boat like a beast of burden, through the dark, silent waters. We slept during the day, covering the boat on shore with tree limbs and debris from the war.

"Sometimes Jabir would explore the shore line for food, scraps, anything to eat or burn for warmth. I would rather be in the boat than to look at the shattered farm lands and villages soaked in blood from the Germans and Russians.

"Jabir told us the Americans were in Germany, to the west. 'The Americans will feed us, give us a roof over our heads, jobs. The Americans . . .'

"The Americans were a people I only knew in a feverish prayer, floating in the Danube, a world between the living and the dead."

She began to cry. The three of us, Kelly, Carl and I, stood up from our chairs, encasing her in the security of our bodies. I touched her shoulders and smoothed her hands clasped tightly. I said her name again and again, "Leona, Leona. We love you, Leona."

"We crawled to the American soldiers. We crawled every inch of the way, eating whatever we could find. Then our luck began to change. A farmer gave us shelter in a barn in return for work on his farm. Every day we dug in the dirt with our fingers, searching for even the smallest potato left behind by the farmer. At night, we lay in the barn, dirty and exhausted, but a roof was over our heads. I knew Jabir and Aliz could not afford to keep me. I also knew there'd be work for me in Fürstenfeldbruck, feeding soldiers, washing their clothes, and shining their shoes. The soldiers were the only ones who had money, so that is where I went, to Fürstenfeldbruck, leaving that little family I loved so well.

"After a few years, I began working in the guest houses, where the soldiers would meet for beer and food in the evenings. That is where I met Albert. We were married there, in Fürstenfeldbruck.

I was sixteen years old. We were good to each other. He brought me to Texas and gave me a home with everything you can image in it, all for me. He loved me, but I could never give him a child. Two miscarriages and we stopped breaking our hearts with the thought of a family.

"Why bring a baby into this hateful world? No, I gave up. I wasn't meant to carry a baby in my womb. Maybe it's because I didn't carry any food in my stomach when I was growing up. Can't nurture a fetus on muscle, bone and tissue nourished by watery soup made from the bones of horses. That's all I knew, all my life. I am a refugee who married an American GI. I learned to manage. A little happiness from flowers and good food, but I learned, I learned never to love anything that can't breathe."

No one spoke for a long while. We remained standing next to her. I reached for her hand and held it in mine, tightly.

"Let's sit down and finish this bottle. It's Christmas, y'all," Kelly said, standing to pour full snifters of Napoleon Brandy that coated our throats with a thick, deep warmth. We drank smiling at each other and singing to the Christmas music that floated out the patio door from the speaker in the living room. "God Rest Ye Merry Gentlemen" floated to our little table, across the St. Augustine grass, through the enormous limbs of the oak tree, and over the six-foot wooden fence, out into the expanse of Houston, a million light-years away from twentieth-century Budapest.

Chapter Sixteen
"We'll take a cup of kindness yet, for Auld Lang Syne."

Leona, Ms. Etiquette herself, could not enjoy someone's hospitality without the immediate need to reciprocate. Our little group met at Leona's for another wonderful meal after Christmas. She insisted on cooking for us as a thank you for Kelly's dinner. She delivered a beautiful pork roast, scalloped potatoes, pickled beets, cucumber and dill salad, and red cabbage. Dessert was served with Amaretto, coffee, and Christmas stollen, wrapped in a linen cloth to preserve the rum-massaged fruit and nut bread.

Following dinner, a three-hour marathon of Canasta occurred with Leona in the driver's seat as hostess and card shark. She was happy. Carl ate like a king. Kelly and I had a night out without wearing makeup and Spanx. By all accounts, we headed into the new year with optimism.

Kelly and I followed our vacation schedule and arrived at the condo, etched into the white limestone hills of Lake Travis, early on New Year's Eve. A cold front dropped the temperatures to the low forties with a chilling driving rain.

I sent Tiffany a text that I'd love to have lunch after I unpacked at the condo. Her response was quick and direct: "Meet me@ work, Ink & Juice, 349 Guadalupe."

It took me nearly an hour to drive into the city. I parked in front of the business, which wasn't much more than a glass door surrounded by cinder block walls. The entire day and the building through the Jeep windshield were gray.

I stepped out of the Jeep into a rain puddle and slid my way into the front door of the Ink & Juice. Tiffany stood behind a plywood bar painted purple. She had cut off all her hair. Short. Military short, buzzed around the ears. The cut was too severe to be considered artsy or post-punk, even by Austin standards. She looked like she was dying of a terminal disease.

I stood there staring at her, and all I could think of was Tiffany at four, sitting on my lap at my vanity, while I put on makeup, as the sun came through the window. Long, long ago, when I was still married and Tiffany's hair was a curly mass of strawberry blond highlights. I never closed the curtains in those days. There was nothing to hide or fear then. All I knew of the outside world was the Bartlett Pear Tree, just beyond the window, alive in white blossoms in the spring.

I stared at her too long with my mouth wide open to make a quick recovery. She knew what I thought. Her face was red.

"Hi, honey," I announced to her and the five-foot half-wit with two full sleeves and a nose ring standing next to her. It obviously was Jared. The impulse to choke him immediately was overwhelming. I clung to Tiffany until it passed.

"Karen, meet Jared," she said, pulling away from me.

"Hey," he grunted.

"Hi, Jared. I've heard so much about you. Glad we're finally meeting." NOT screamed inside my head. Sticky note to self: vet Jared on social media.

I swear I heard him say, "May I offer you a tattoo and a glass of carrot juice?"

Tiffany and I ate a late lunch at Maria's Empanadas on Sixth Street. We walked from the Ink & Juice under an umbrella, both rejuvenated by the north wind pushing us along the sidewalk.

"Let's get this out of the way before lunch. I know you hate my hair, just don't say anything about it. Ever. Now that that's out of the way, how are you doing?"

"Yes. Well, I'm not going to say anything about your hair

since you put it to me that way. I see we're going to be polite about all this, so yes, I'm all right. Really. Glad to be here," I laughed, pulling her closer to me as we entered the restaurant.

"Let me order for us, Karen. You'll love it."

The waitress appeared and Tiffany, confidant in her Austin-urban cool, didn't look at the menu, but allowed her desire to roll off her empanada-connoisseur tongue, "We'll have six of the Peruvian empanadas with grass-fed beef, onions, raisins, olives and hard cooked eggs. Bring us two agua de fresas. For dessert, black coffee with two apricot filled empanadas."

"Sounds wonderful."

"Yeah, it's fresh."

"A reprise from my microwave diet. Lovely. Hey, don't let me forget, I've got some gifts for you and Jared in the car."

"You don't like him. That's obvious. You've never had much of a poker face."

"Don't make too much of that. No one would be good enough."

"He's not so bad. He was a medical tech in Albuquerque at a private, very exclusive rehab, before moving to Austin."

"Wow. That's a wide berth. Medical tech to tattoo artist."

"Come on."

"You're right. Let's enjoy our time together."

She stared at her nails, pulling at the half-inch ragged cuticle hanging on her left thumb. It began to bleed.

"He's got beautiful handwriting, almost like calligraphy," she offered, wiping the blood off her thumb with her dinner napkin.

"Oh. How about that." I wanted it to be rude. She sold out to a half-wit. Before me was a girl who loved poetry, flowers, and furry animals. The image of that girl, twelve years old reciting poetry every morning before school, was lost somewhere in the butchered haircut, nose ring, and defeated funk in front of me. I closed my eyes and welcomed that long-ago image. I heard her perfectly parted rose lips delivering each word of William Carlos Williams' "The Red Wheelbarrow" with such enunciation, it made me cry. It happened every morning at the kitchen table with a bowl of cereal and me as the privileged audience.

The Red Wheelbarrow

so much depends
upon

a red wheel
barrow

glazed with rain
water

beside the white
chickens.

A heavy sigh escaped from me.

"Karen, where are you?"

"I'm in our kitchen, in Houston, about seven years ago. It's easier for me right now."

"Look. You need to like him. I haven't had a period in six weeks."

Just like that the entire world changed. Just like that every hope, every dream I ever had for her was laid at the feet of Jared, the medical tech-turned-tattoo artist. *Don't say anything stupid, don't do it.* The waitress put a platter of food before us, with two sunny little drinks afloat with strawberries. *Did she sleep with him the first night they met? Oh, God. Did I not teach her anything in the years she lived with me? She could be pregnant with a bloodstream full of Adderall.*

I reached across the table and touched her hand.

"Do you love him?"

"I don't know. He's the first guy who showed up when he said he would. Is that love?"

"Oh, honey." The tears came. I tried to hide them, but her

utter lack of self-esteem broke my heart. I could have carried her out of there in my arms, back to the Jeep, and back to our home in Houston, with Poncho and Max.

"Just help me, Karen. Don't judge me or Jared."

"Of course I will."

"I haven't told him yet. Actually, the pee test kit is on the grocery list."

"Let's do it now. I'll get the groceries you need."

She looked at me, took a bite of the Peruvian Empanada, and nodded.

She sat in the car while I picked up bananas, Greek yogurt, organic milk, and a pregnancy test kit at the Kroger on Guadalupe. When I got back to the car, she was texting.

"You okay?"

"Just letting Jared know I'm not feeling well, going home."

"Good. I'll make us some tea and you can rest."

"No, just drop me off. I'll do the kit and let you know."

My heart sank. Somehow, I had pushed her completely out of my life. It's because I always overreacted. She just didn't want me around.

"I don't even know where you live. Now, that's a real shame."

"It is what it is, Karen. Don't make any more out of it. Call you in a few hours. I'm probably gonna nap."

I dropped her off in front of a cinder block apartment complex with one dead palm tree in the dying grass near the office. It was about half a mile from the Ink & Juice. She probably walked that route several times a day. I sat in the car with the wiper blades slapping the windshield, watching her walk in the rain to the second floor of the complex, soaking wet, thin, pale, and pregnant. I knew it. She didn't need a kit to tell her that. I felt it like an anvil on my chest.

Being the neurotic middle-aged woman I am, I searched for a nail tech salon before heading back to the condo. I didn't want to bring my angst to Kelly, so I thought I'd stew, while some poor

Vietnamese woman sawed on my toes, hating me for being an American girl-woman. There's that label again. Maybe that's just who I am.

It was another dimly lit, cinder block building with a flat, low roof, painted purple. Are there any buildings in this town built with anything else? The more diversity Austin claimed, the more same old same old I saw. Hey, if you must keep shouting to the world you're unique, well, maybe you're not so unique after all.

The minute I walked in, a middle-aged Vietnamese man looked directly at the woman in the white smock, who jumped up, turned the water faucet on at the base of the pedicure chair, then pushed me in it. I hate these places. They make me depressed. How was I to know the guy wasn't cursing her in Vietnamese? His tone was angry. I felt I was causing trouble for some poor woman, cleaning people's feet for minimum wage, whenever I walked through the door.

"Pick color. Pick color."

I got up and walked to a painted plywood rack of nail polish on the wall.

"How about this? *I'm Not a Waitress Red.*" I laughed out loud, reading the name of the nail polish. She grabbed the bottle of blood red lacquer out of my hand and moved toward the pedicure chair.

Pushing me into the chair, she removed my shoes and forced both feet into a swirling array of warm water and bubbles. She handed me a magazine and walked back to the pedicure station.

The magazine laid unopened in my lap. I closed my eyes and prayed for Tiffany. For her happiness, for a decent chance in this world, for some peace of mind.

"Why so sad, lady? It's New Year's Eve."

She was back, sitting on a tiny stool at my feet. She took one foot in her hand and began feverishly scrubbing my calluses.

"I'm Nanh. Why you don't want mani too? Look pretty for tonight," she announced behind my raised right foot.

"No. Nothing going on tonight. I usually overeat, drink, and fall asleep before the ball drops in New York City."

"Lots of bars, music. You go."

"The thought of ruining my buzz talking to strangers is defeating."

She looked up and laughed at me. The mini wind chimes tied to the glass front door rang, and a pregnant woman walked in. A look of concern flashed across Nanh's face. She put my right foot back in the water and approached the woman.

"Mani? Pedi?"

"Both. I'm due any minute. I deserve the works."

"Sit here," Nanh motioned to the manicure station. "Chung do your nails."

The pregnant woman collapsed in a black vinyl, swivel chair on wheels. She drank slowly from a straw in a large Styrofoam cup from the stop-and-rob convenience store on the corner of Sixth and Guadalupe. She set the cup on the floor next to her purse. It was difficult to guess her age from where I was sitting. Early thirties? She was an attractive woman, but not naturally pretty. Like a lot of women, she learned a long time ago how to make the most of what she had through the magic of cosmetics.

Nanh returned to the swirl of bubbling water and my feet. She grabbed the left foot and began scrubbing, but not with as much intensity as she had before. She kept her back to Chung and the other customer.

We were a strange party for New Year's Eve. Why not have a little conversation?

While Nanh was drying both feet and rubbing my legs down with a vat of pink lotion, I called across to the woman with the Styrofoam cup at her feet.

"When is your baby due?"

"Actually, I'm a week late."

"Exciting! Is this your first child?"

"No, I got three already; I'm not keeping this one." She bent down to pick up the Styrofoam cup and drank quickly from the straw. She looked at me while she was drinking, then turned around to face Chung, as he removed the dry cuticles from her nail base with a mini sander.

And that was that. I felt like she just told me off. My skin felt hot and my hands were shaking. Her response to my question lacked any emotion, as if she were declining the larger fries in the burger meal deal.

Don't judge her, Karen. You don't even know the whole story. She may be a surrogate mother for some poor woman who can't get pregnant.

"Nanh, I'll take a mani, too." Where else was I to go in the rain on New Year's Eve with my Tiffany in a crappy apartment, staring at a pee test strip, wondering if what she saw was really what she saw.

Nanh stood up from her little stool and grabbed the nail polish. She sat back down, sighed heavily, then began applying it to my toes. I studied her bent head for a while. She was probably first generation Vietnamese-American, so she had to be in her late forties, maybe early fifties. Her hair was like a black and white silk rope against milk white skin. Beautiful. She had a small frame with hands and fingers the size of a child's.

"How long have you lived in Austin, Nanh?"

"Came here after school. Like a lot of Vietnamese people, I grew up on coast, Port Aransas. My dad was shrimper. Had boat with brothers. My mom got beautician's license; I did too. Okay money. Chung, my husband. We opened shop two years ago."

"Guess there's more money in nails than hair."

"Sometimes."

The pregnant woman stood up from the mani table and picked up her Styrofoam cup.

"That's it, man. My back is killing me." She reached into her purse and paid Chung with three ten-dollar bills. "Keep the rest."

And with a tingle from the cheap wind chimes at the glass door entrance, she left.

Nanh looked at Chung, then at me.

"She good customer. Been coming long time with her mother and grandmother. Her mother mad at her for not keeping baby. Her mother keep her other children, two boys, girl still in diapers."

Was this some kind of a test from God? This pregnant woman with the Big Gulp drink and Tiffany's possible pregnancy all in the same afternoon?

With my pedi complete, Nanh tilted a mini-fan on my toes for drying.

"My dad dead. My mom old, still working. I send money to Vietnam to help our family, like they did, every month. People are poor there. Fat girl drinking forty-eight-ounce Coke getting nails done, says she can't afford a baby."

Chung yelled something in Vietnamese to Nanh. She responded in Vietnamese, with the same rapid-fire, angry tone he used. She turned to me with a pair of thin, cheap flip flops in her hands.

"This country rich—free education, free health care, free food, free diapers. Her mom help her. She don't want. My country, very poor. People keep babies. Family help. Don't understand, but I don't say anything. None of my business. People crazy in this country."

With that, she placed my feet in the flip flops and escorted me to the swivel chair in front of Chung.

"Pay now, won't ruin nails." Those were the last words I heard from Nanh.

I was in Chung's world now.

With *I'm Not a Waitress Red* on my hands and feet, I walked to Lone Star Liquor, west on Sixth street, near the Market District. I found the cold rain refreshing after the nail salon. I picked up two mini bottles of whiskey—the fast food approach to shots of courage. I walked back to where I parked the Jeep, slid in, and poured both bottles of Jameson down my throat, watching the rain slide across the windshield. I thought of Tiffany in the apartment or out walking in the rain, searching for another home pregnancy kit she had purchased with tip jar money from the Ink & Juice. Maybe a different kit would hold a different result.

Once the liquid warmth soothed my nerves, I called Leona.

"Hey neighbor" poured out of me when she picked up on the second ring.

"Happy New Year, Karen. Max and Poncho send their regards."

"Oh, that's great. I'm glad everyone is getting along."

"Yes, of course. We are doing well. And you? Tiffany?" Leona had always pronounced her name with three distinct syllables, not the slur of a name with two syllables. She said it like she was a jewel; my precious jewel, Tiffany.

"Leona, pray for us. Pray for my girl. She is not good, not one bit good. Her hair is chopped up, crazy clothes, crazy jewelry. It's all a big mess, big mess." It rushed out of me, leaving me woozy from the whiskey and the emotion.

"Oh for God's sake, Karen. Are you drinking?"

"Does it matter? Does it matter, Leona? Be my friend right now, not my conscience."

"Stop drinking and get a hold of yourself."

With that I did a quick look in the rearview mirror. She was right. I looked as crazy as I sounded. I took a deep breath.

"Is Kelly there with you?'

"I'm headed back to be with her. It will be all right. I can handle this."

"Of course, you can handle it."

"Yes, just take care of Poncho and Max. I'll be home in a few days."

"Karen, why did you call me?"

"I guess I wanted you to tell me how to fix it."

"Fix what? Tiffany?"

"Forget it. She will be okay. It just takes time. Lots of time to stop your heart from bleeding all over the place."

"Maybe you should come home."

"No. I'll explain it all when I get back."

"Pray the Rosary, Karen. Our blessed Mother will help you."

I immediately got a visual of the bleeding heart of Jesus picture in Leona's living room.

"I don't need a mother, Leona. I need Tiffany to come home."

"Just look at yourself. Drinking alone, God knows where in Austin. You need a mother."

I hung up and called Kelly. If there was one thing I could count on, it was Kelly answering the phone when I called. I loved that about her.

"Hey, I'm headed back to the condo. Let's go out tonight."

"What happened to you? Is Tiffany okay?

"Am I that predictable? A night on the town doesn't necessarily mean my world is imploding."

"Got it. Whew. Can't wait to bring in the New Year with this new crap."

Chapter Seventeen
A New Year, A New Man

Kelly and I arrived at the Broken Spoke Dance Hall & Saloon on Lamar at 9:00 p.m. Yes, we were early. The place was full of people our age; it was too early for anyone under fifty to show their face.

Kelly was wearing a denim miniskirt and a tee shirt with a picture of Willie Nelson on the front. Beneath it were the words FREE WILLIE. On her feet were red cowboy boots with yellow roses tooled into the leather. I finally got her wardrobe budget. What she didn't spend on shirts, she saved for shoes.

"What's up with the feather in your hair?

"I found it this morning by the post oak. Sign of good luck."

"Indians and Janis Joplin wore feathers. They had terrible luck."

"Lighten up a bit, Karen. Take a pill."

The remark left me speechless, but the look I gave her sent a direct message.

"Okay, let's have a beer, instead," she offered.

The band started playing a Joe Ely tune. It filled the cavernous abyss of the Broken Spoke with an unspoken hope for the divorced, separated, middle-aged, early crowd.

> "I have stumbled on the plains, staggered in the wind
> Stood at a crossroad or two
> Cried to a river, swept to the sea
> All just to get to you.

I have jumped the yellow cab, hopped a rusty freight
Sang till my lips turned blue
Flown a silver bird, from tops of the clouds
All just to get to you.

I ran too hard, I played too rough.
I gave my love, not near enough.
I bled too red, I cried too blue.
I beat my fist against the moon.
All just to get to you."

I was transfixed by every word of the song. I sang the lyrics like a poem, enunciating every word like a universal truth. The singers and songwriters of the world were far removed from the dry decay of the academic poets, slaves to publishing and form. The songwriters' passion, their refusal to play by the rules, was the source of many young girls' hearts, raw with youth and inexperience. That once was my young girl's heart.

What would Joe Ely or Willie Nelson look like in a high school English class, I wondered, taking a long draw from the beer bottle Kelly handed me. I supposed that was the kid in the back row, intense eyes, hiding behind a notebook, drawing boats and horses, roses and daggers, instead of circling the pronouns and underlining the linking verbs on a worksheet.

As I was enjoying my romantic thought looking at the singer in the band, I noticed a man to my right staring at me.

I hate people invading my space in a public place. That's why I *never* went out to bars, except for our little pub in Houston. I returned his look with a faint smile, and here he came, all smiles. *Do you have to be that eager? I really just want to drink my beer and sing out loud by myself.*

"Good band. They do a lot of covers. Pat Green, Lyle Lovett."

"Yes. I particularly like this song," I answered coolly. Kelly smiled at me, then walked away, leaving me with Mr. Congenial. It was either because the guy was too old to hold her attention, or she thought I deserved some male attention all to myself.

"Did I interrupt something?" he asked.

"Oh no, that's just her," I said, staring at Kelly's butt, packed into the denim skirt like sausage casing. "She likes to move around in places like this; she's got the attention span of a gnat."

"Well, would you like to dance before the song is over?"

"Sure," I said, surprising myself. He took the beer bottle out of my hand and placed it on a table behind us. Taking my right hand, he led me to the dance floor. That male touch, someone else in control, literally took my breath away for a moment. He smiled at me with his eyes, dark, deep brown, while pressing his body against mine; his right hand was on my back, his left hand grasping my hand against his chest. We moved in a two-step dance to the music.

It had been a long time, years since I had danced with a man, literally years since I willingly let a man take something from me, and move my body to his, without regret or defense. I never wanted that song to end. I never wanted to know his name. I just wanted to keep dancing, listening to every line of poetry Joe Ely wrote in that song.

> "From the California Shore
> Where the mighty ocean roars
> To the lands of the Hopi and the Sioux
> I walked the desert sands
> Crossed the Rio Grande
> All just to get to you.
>
> I have stumbled on the plains
> Staggered in the wind
> Stood at a crossroad or two
> Cried to a river
> Swept to the sea
> All just to get to you."

Then it was over. The music stopped. The man's body pulled away from me, but he held on to my hand, walking me across the dance floor to where we had stood before. He reached for my beer bottle and handed it to me.

"Can I buy you another beer?" he asked.

"Sure." Another one syllable reply. *Who was this guy?*

I felt my purse buzz against my right side. I dug in to find my cell phone. I was immediately back into my world of blind-sided anxiety, when I read the text from Tiffany.

"Brunch tomorrow, 11, black-eyed peas, cabbage, ham, corn-bread, apt. 216."

"How are you?"

She texted back an emoticon of a smiley face. What was that supposed to mean? No time to figure that out; mystery man was heading my way with two longnecks in his hands.

"What's your name?" he asked, handing me a beer.

"Karen. I'm from Houston, here for the holiday visiting family."

"Footloose."

"What?"

"My name's Footloose. Like the movie, the song."

"Now there's a story behind that nickname."

He took a sip from his beer, all the while looking at me, gauging my interest in him.

"Lost a foot in the Nineties. The nickname stuck."

"You say it as if you misplaced it somewhere. What happened?"

"Desert Storm. Now, don't get weird on me. What's a foot? If the name is too much for you, the birth certificate says Matt Broussard."

I laughed and felt my face turn hot. I did a quick glance around the area—no sight of Kelly.

"What do you do for a living, Karen?"

"I'm a high school English teacher. Nothing else but teach."

"Do you like it?"

"Yes, I do. Not many teachers can say that. I actually love my students."

"Probably why you've never done anything else. It fits too good."

"That or I'm a creature of habit." I took a long draw from my beer.

"Ms. English teacher, do you also write creatively?"

"I love writers, of course. I have my favorites, but I don't quite have the time or discipline to write. Wish I did. Someday. Do you write?"

"Yeah, every day now. I mean, I wanted to for a long time, but stuff got in the way. Guess I was just doing research. Was in the military, retired, so I moved to Austin and started an MFA at UT. I'll graduate this spring."

"What's your genre?"

"Southern Grit; ugly small-town sagas, much uglier than Flannery O'Connor."

"Oh my God, I never heard that term before. It's hilarious."

"Visualize meth trailers and tattoo-covered bar maids."

"Got it. Is that where you've done all your research, bars and trailer houses?"

"Some of it." He laughed, refusing to be insulted by my smart aleck remark. "Now, aren't you going to ask me if you can read my work?"

"Can I read your work?"

He laughed and grabbed my hand and pulled me out to the dance floor. Twin violins began the opening of "Amarillo by Morning." It echoed through the hall, reminding me of a time when I danced with my father in the kitchen, holding tightly to his arms, with my feet on top of his, as he balanced us in a two-step pattern.

Footloose followed the tradition, singing in my ear as we danced. I couldn't figure out if he was that confident or this was a part of his act. Could be he just loved the song and this was part of a joyful outburst on his part, or he thought he had a sexy voice and he was luring me in. Weird.

The band repeated the chorus, as he led me through a dramatic spin, steering us away from the other legs and elbows on the dance floor. "George Strait never gets old," he laughed and squeezed me tightly against him. The band didn't stop to rest, but immediately launched into the opening guitar chords of Willie Nelson's "Angel Flying Too Close to the Ground."

I did it. I held on to a stranger, this man I had only met minutes before, as if I had known him all my life. The seductive illusion of abandonment to a total stranger coursed through every vein in my body. I felt his body move perfectly against mine, as I closed my eyes to everything in my head and all around me. When the music stopped, we remained holding each other on the dance floor, until embarrassed, I pulled away, searching for Kelly and an exit.

"You okay?" Matt handed me my beer.

I took it and looked toward the bar, where Kelly was holding court. From where I was standing, it looked like Kelly was flirting with a fraternity house of twenty year olds. I knew then it would be a short night. We'd never make it to midnight, much less the ride back to the condo if I didn't play the grown-up. I didn't want the night to end, but I knew from experience that short and sweet resounded far better in the morning than a wee hour regret.

The song ended. Hand-in-hand we walked off the dance floor.

"Matt, I hate to end the night. You've been a lot of fun. I've got some family obligations early tomorrow."

"When you going back to Houston?"

"I got another day with family duties, then it's back to Houston. But hey, I'd love to read your trashy novel."

"Good, you're interested. Give me your email. I'll send it to you."

I wrote it down on the back of a grocery store receipt I found in my purse.

He reached out to hug me, and I soaked every bit of him into my skin, as if I hadn't had a breath of fresh air or the touch of a man for years.

"Please don't correct my manuscript in red, Ms. English teacher. I don't think I can take that," he laughed, pulling away from me.

"No guarantees," I smiled, turning to walk away from him, wondering if he were watching me walk, what my butt looked like in jeans, and if I stumbled and swayed while walking.

I approached the bar and it was true to form—a gathering of bar flies with Kelly in the center.

"Hey, girrrlll, you finally decided to sit this one out?"

"Time to go."

"One more for the road, Karen. Come on, it's New Year's."

This remark was met by a round of approval from her young pages.

I picked up her purse and gently pushed her right elbow, leading her off the barstool onto her feet.

"Good night, boys. We'll see you next time we're in town." She was met with another rowdy round of cat calls, whistles, and 'We love you, Kel-leeee.'"

We put our arms around each other's waists as our shoes crunched against the gravel parking lot of the Broken Spoke.

"I'm shocked, even by your standards, hitting the undergrad crowd."

"Karen, ever heard the lyrics, 'Love the one you're with?'"

"Hand me the car keys and get in the car."

It was almost midnight when we pulled into the parking structure at the condo.

We got out and walked to the street, where a small opening between the tree canopy showed a sliver of moon. We held hands as we looked up at the slight moon, loving each other and the friendship that had endured the passing of time and the melancholy of a new year.

"Oh God, forgive us our faults, our selfishness, our small hearts. We pray for a better year."

Kelly sighed and squeezed my hand locked in hers.

Chapter Eighteen
And Baby Makes Three

I knew what the year would hold for me and Tiffany when I walked through the front door of apartment 216 and saw the cardboard *papier-mâché* stork centered on the coffee table. Were we really going to celebrate this? I was sick to my stomach and felt the crawling of a massive tension headache making its way from my neck to the center of my forehead. *Don't say anything! Keep your mouth shut! Put a smile on your face and sit down at the table.*

The stork left Kelly speechless as well as she greeted Tiffany with a faint smile and slumped shoulders. The rhinestone tiara Kelly wore in celebration of New Year revelry slumped to the back of her head, then fell on the shag carpeting at her feet. We were all defeated by the sign of the stork.

The proud daddy stood in front of an electric stove frying bacon. I could kill him. I could just pick up that cast iron skillet and knock him cold, leaving a dent and some bacon grease on his Neanderthal sloped forehead. *Control yourself or you'll lose her forever.*

"I like to put bacon in my cornbread batter. Adds a nice crunch."

God help me. It speaks. After that, the lid was off the box for me.

"Tiffany, why is there a stork on the table?"

She looked at me with the saddest eyes, sad beyond the eyes of a college freshman. She had entered the world of women with broken hearts.

"Are you pregnant?"

Jared turned from the grease to face me. "We're having a baby."

I grabbed my girl. I grabbed her with all the love that was in my very being.

"I'm happy for you, honey," I lied.

Kelly got up from the couch and hugged her. "I'm going to throw you the biggest baby shower!" True to Kelly, always making chicken salad out of chicken poop.

The three of us, three women, mother-daughter-friend, made an unbreakable circle with our bodies enfolding into each other; we were the wagons in the circle against HIM. *You are not welcome in this family. You will never be a part of this group.*

"Let's open the champagne," Jared sang out. Out of the fridge he produced a $4 bottle of pink champagne. He popped the cork and filled four glasses of hangover until they fizzed over onto the counter top.

"To my woman and child."

We raised our plastic glasses to Tiffany, who stood before us, tiny, pale, and sad. The only one happy was Jared, as if this little gathering was about him. He had just added a new skill to his resume—stud services. As if that made him a man—as if he were qualified to be a father.

"You ladies just chill in the living room with your drinks. I'm about to get the ham, greens, and black-eyed peas on the table."

"Thanks, Jared. I can hardly wait," I snapped, leading Tiffany and Kelly to the loveseat perched on bricks, obviously stolen from the meager landscaping of the apartment complex. The only comfort that piece of furniture offered was my mother's handmade quilt covering the cigarette holes in the plaid upholstery.

The three of us sat, side-by-side.

"I never gave you your Christmas present. Got it right here in my purse."

I handed her a small box wrapped in forest green paper with a red ribbon. Tiffany smiled, the first smile I had seen in a long time. She pulled a thin gold chain with a cross pendant from the box. She turned to hug me; it was then that the tears came, falling into the enclosure of my arms wrapped around her.

"You're not alone in this, Tiffany."

"I let you down, school, the whole thing. One lousy semester at UT and the whole world changed. From school girl to momma in less than 120 days."

"You can still go to school. Just take care of you right now. But listen to me. Please, I am begging you, please don't marry this man."

"He loves me, Karen."

I shut my mouth and pulled away. But I had one more thing to say, one more. I couldn't help myself. I might not get this chance again with Jared serving up the goods in the kitchen. This could be the last supper, especially where Jared was concerned. I wasn't wasting any second I had with her.

"Tiffany, are you still taking Adderall?"

"Stopped yesterday, when I found out I was pregnant."

"You'll need good prenatal care."

"There's a clinic on Congress Avenue. I can go there."

"You need good care."

"Stop. This is all I can do for right now, Karen. Just stop."

As if on cue, Jared spread his arms, touching both sides of the kitchen and living room entrance, flexing his inked shoulder muscles in a display of manhood. It couldn't be for our benefit, but only his, as he beamed radiantly, "Ladies, food's on!"

"You can come home, right now, with me."

"This is my home, Karen." A thousand NOs screamed inside my head.

I ignored her and the speeding train barreling down our throats in the next few months. I decided to concentrate on Jared. Grabbing my purse, I searched for his Christmas gift somewhere on the bottom with loose coins and candy wrappers.

"I almost forgot," I said, smiling at him. "Here's a little Christmas gift I picked up for you."

I handed him the unwrapped paperback, reading the cover out loud, *How to Win Friends and Influence People* by Dale Carnegie. "It's a classic for up-and-coming people in the world." With that, I sat at the head of the table in the kitchen, ladled out three heaping spoons of black-eyed peas and raised my pink champagne glass as a toast. "Southern folklore says black-eyed peas eaten on New Year's Day will bring good luck. Everybody eat a bunch; we need all the luck we can get."

Chapter Nineteen
The Monkey Bar Queen

As soon as we got in the car, Kelly started.

"You really didn't have to take the air out of the room, Karen. Everyone was already miserable, well, Jared was happy, but he doesn't count. Why didn't you just play it cool with Tiffany? You put her between a rock and a hard place. Of course, she chose the hard place –Jared."

"I did it because I was wild with anger, hurt, at him, at her, at myself for not being in better contact with her."

"You don't have to make it worse by alienating him or her."

"This isn't Tiffany. This is just not who she is. She's better, stronger than to take up with a bottom feeder. She's overcome so much, even as a little girl when she figured out her mother wasn't coming back for her. I don't even have the words . . . she was a fighter. Did I ever tell you how she mastered the monkey bars in fourth grade?"

Kelly smiled at me, pushed her seat into a reclining position, and closed her eyes. I didn't care if she listened. I wanted to remember by myself, to relish each picture in my memory, speak it out loud, like a fable of a sad, little girl whose mother didn't want her. So, the little girl ate and ate, creating a barrier of her own flesh against anyone ever hurting her again. Then the day came for change in the little girl's world.

The Monkey Bar Queen: A Fable of Self Worth

Once upon a time, there was a little girl in the fourth grade at Lincoln Elementary School. She was a heavy-set little girl, known to her classmates as Chubs.

Chubs accepted her fate and became the funny, chubby girl who was not a threat to anyone, so she always had lots of friends. Deep inside she knew she was much more than this, but she lacked the courage to be anything else than what her peers labeled her. It all came to a screeching halt when the winds of change prompted the physical education teacher to schedule the fourth grade physical fitness test.

The first test of endurance for the fourth graders was the monkey bars. This high wire of eight aluminum rungs was the first test to prove their upper body strength to the teacher and their peers. Below it was the pit of failure, a combination of sand and wood chips waiting for the victim, who despite sweat, strain, and peer pressure, dropped in a puff of disappointment to the ground.

The little girl watched each participant in front of her. She desperately searched the eyes of the achievers, seeking clues for success. All the while, she prayed that God would deliver a thunderstorm so severe all the children would have to run inside the gym and the physical fitness test would be cancelled. Her prayers were unanswered. It was now her turn in line.

She made it halfway across, her arms trembling as she extended one arm to the next rung. Hanging between the two rungs, her strength gave out and she fell to the ground below. From on top the wood chips, bruised and humiliated, she was told to hurry and get in line for the softball throw.

She would be tested again on the monkey bars in two weeks.

From the back of the line at the softball throw, she faced her crossroads. She could either be Chubs or the Monkey Bar Queen. Monkey Bar Queen. What a wondrous image that conjured! Beautiful. Powerful. Confident.

"Yes, I will be the Monkey Bar Queen!"

The little girl didn't tell her aunt about her failure to pass the fourth grade fitness test; instead, every day after school, she went to the playground and practiced, over, and over, and over again until she could master the monkey bars. She did. She received a certificate with a gold seal and a blue ribbon for "Excellence Achieved in Physical Fitness." But the real success, which no one or anything could ever take from her, was self–discovery. Forever, the Monkey Bar Queen!

No one called her Chubs anymore. They called her Tiffany, like the beautiful jewelry store, filled with rare jewels, diamonds and pearls, jewelry worthy of a queen! No one could ever make her feel hopeless. She knew change was possible with focus, faith, and determination. She didn't have to pretend to be someone she wasn't, so others would like her. She didn't have to accept anything less than the best! Because no matter what life would bring her, no matter what people may say about her, she knew she was the Monkey Bar Queen. She didn't need a safety net!

I hit the 610 Loop in Houston, and Kelly woke up, while inside my head I chanted the prayer of the desperate, *Please God, please don't let anything hurt Tiffany or her little baby. I'll give you my life, Lord. It's yours. If only, this one time, you'll do this for me. I'll do anything for you.* Sticky note to self: go to Mass every day starting tomorrow.

Chapter Twenty
Sweet Dream Baby

School started with the winter blues for faculty and students at Heights Central High School. If it wasn't raining, a massive yellow haze floated in the sky courtesy of the petro-chemical plants east of town. The best we could do as a collective was soldier on until Martin Luther King Day, our first federal holiday.

There wasn't much eye contact and a lot of silent reading in the lesson plan the first week back to school. I didn't want to interact and neither did they. We all wanted to be elsewhere.

The after-Christmas line of demarcation for the haves and have-nots was quite clear the first week of school. The haves were wearing new clothes, shoes, and jewelry. They carried expensive purses and backpacks, while the have-nots hid in the massive folds of the tee shirts they got as a consolation prize for participating in a blood drive, a food drive, or a marketing plan for a local car dealership.

Principal Kenny roamed the halls that week, searching for exposed belly buttons, red bra straps and boys' boxers providing buttock coverage for pants slung too low. "Someone throw him a bone," deadpanned Joel Perez, sharpening his pencil near the door while staring out its rectangle pane of glass.

God, I loved that kid, but I played the teacher.

"Okay class, let's go over "'Mediation XVII.'"

A blank look covered the faces in front of me, but that wasn't unusual for my second block class.

"John Donne, the English poet. You read him yesterday. 'No man is an island . . . ,' John Donne."

I heard a collective moan, but it might have been in my head.

Exodus Brown, an old soul stuck in a seventeen-year-old body, looked at me. Her ink pen was stuck behind her right ear in a circular mass of hair that appeared as a black halo found in a Raphael orthodox icon. I never knew what would come out of her mouth, but I did know she was smart, smart beyond her years, and every time I spoke her name, I thought of the woman who named her, a mother, who believed in the power of a name.

"Exodus?"

She was weighing the thought of whether she should contribute to the conversation. It was a calculated risk—either she'd alienate herself from the other girls for showing off or the boys would consider her intelligence a threat.

"I didn't know if the poet wanted to connect everybody through the images of the church bell, with us being all God's children, or the bell was an alarm, waking people from their selfishness; a warning to humanity that no one stands alone; we're all connected. Everything I do may affect somebody else."

Beautiful, beautiful Exodus.

"Excellent. That is exactly what he wrote about."

It became a literary discussion between me and Exodus. Occasionally Joel would add a word or two on imagery. It didn't matter. I never expected everyone to get it; I was overjoyed Exodus and Joel did. There's hope even in the winter within a city that had lost its charm for me a long time ago.

My friendship with Leona grew in its intimacy following the weekend in Austin. She invited me over after work Friday evening and included Poncho and Max. They became a part of the gathering, resting at our feet in Leona's doily-induced dining room, where I'd occasionally slip Max a delicacy from the table. It was the perfect human-animal encounter, human fingers clenching meat connect with dog's teeth, all underneath the cloak of a starched white tablecloth.

Leona's time with Poncho and Max dismissed her former belief that animals in the house were breeders of disease and filth. That was the old Leona, and in many ways I was changing too. But I don't think for the better.

"Every second of every minute I've wanted to drive to Austin and drag Tiffany kicking and screaming back here. But that's not going to work. I'm too exhausted and overwhelmed by everything to think of anything better."

"You must give this time, Karen. It's only been a few weeks."

"I have to be diligent, Leona. That's what I've always been with her. Never once letting my guard down, except this one time, she leaves home and I assume I can live my own life, and she'll be okay. Well, look what that brought. A few months of letting go and she's covered in tattoos, pregnant, and living in a low-rent apartment in east Austin."

Draining the wine glass, I poured another. No four-or-six-ounce question here. I filled it to the rim. Leona gave me the stink eye then began clearing the table. So, this was her routine when she didn't like something I said or did.

"Leona, come back in here. I'll stop drinking if that's what's upsetting you. Here, I'm bringing the bottle back to the kitchen for you."

I got up and followed her into the kitchen. She took the bottle from me.

"You need to stop drinking. You are not a foolish woman, Karen. You are an educated woman. A good woman. The fact Tiffany is pregnant is not the end of the world. Life can be much worse. Your drinking will make it much worse."

"You're right. I know that, but tell me how to stop my heart from breaking. Tell me. You don't stop caring when your child moves out."

"Let's have some coffee and dessert." She removed a glass dome over a crystal cake plate and smiled at me. "*Almás Pite*, Hungarian apple cake."

She sliced two generous portions and plugged in the percolator. I stood watching her, like a girl-woman, an American girl-woman, crying and slightly drunk.

"Come. Sit down here." I followed her back to the dining room, where she placed a dessert plate and a cup of coffee before me.

"We will bring Tiffany home, Karen. But you must pray and you must be patient or you will lose her forever. She thinks she loves this man, this Jared. You must wait for her to discover she doesn't love him, at all." She picked up the creamer on the table and poured velvety, thick cream into the black coffee in front of me. "You must remember. We are smarter than Jared, but more importantly, you love her more than Jared ever will."

I spent the rest of the evening listening to her, eating the cake, and drinking coffee. When I got up to leave, she handed me a piece of the apple cake wrapped in wax paper and a meat bone in aluminum foil.

"For breakfast. The bone is from the roast; that's for the good boy, Max," She bent down and scratched beneath his right ear. "You, Poncho, there's nothing tonight." Poncho released an indignant meow and ran to the front door.

When I got home, there was a missed call from Tiffany on my cell phone and a Facebook friend request from Matt Broussard. It was after 10:00 p.m. Too late to call, so I sent Tiffany a text I would call in the morning around nine. Before I turned out the light and closed my eyes, I accepted the friend request from Matthew Broussard.

Sweet dream baby, Mr. Matt Broussard. Mystery man, let me dream of you, whether it is who you really are or who I want you to be. Let me dream of dancing. You pressing your body against mine, while the lights and the music circle around my head. Your eyes and your smile tell me I can believe that maybe, maybe this time I'll get it right. Maybe I wasn't meant to sleep alone for the next thirty years. When I'm dancing with you, the possibilities of you and me, heart to heart, are eternal, like a thousand New Year's Eves, promising a better tomorrow.

*   *   *

Saturday morning, I sat staring out the front window, sitting on the couch with Max and Poncho. It was raining hard with occasional flashes of lighting in the early morning light. Puddles of water stood in the street and in the yard. Leona's yard once full of pink hibiscus, purple begonias, and white azaleas, was now dormant and grey. I called Tiffany's cell. She answered on the second ring.

"Sorry I didn't get back to you last night. I was just tired from the first week back at school."

"No problem. Hey, I'll have to keep this short, I'm at work. But I got a prenatal appointment at the clinic nearby. Thought it would make you happy if I let you know I'm being a responsible mom."

"That's great. How are you feeling?"

"Tired. I'm still trying to take a few classes this semester, get the history and science requirements out of the way."

"Please do, Tiff. Don't give up on school. Do you need some money?"

"I always need money, but I don't want to fight about it."

"Text me your address. I know I should remember it, but I got to write everything down these days. I'll send a check; no fighting required."

"Thank you. Things are moving along with Jared. You shouldn't worry. Lots of women have lots of babies every day. Remember how much I loved the stories by Pearl S. Buck when I was in middle school—*The Good Earth*. Those were real women, harvesting rice, having babies and tying them to their backs to keep working."

"Yes, I remember. You'd read in your room at night with a flashflight, long after I told you to go to bed. I never stopped you, because I knew how much you were enjoying yourself. Books in bed, nothing better."

"Right. Well, got to go, customers here. I'll let you know what the doc says, okay."

"Love you, hon. Take care of yourself."

The phone went dead. I drank coffee for another hour, sitting on the couch, staring out the window. I tried to imagine what Tiffany would look like in six months. It was such an alien thought for me. A baby in her womb, when mine laid fallow all these years. I had wanted children at one time. I wanted children with Greg those first hopeful years of marriage. Like so many things in the past, I just let it go. I never met anyone who was worth the risk of marrying again.

Were you for real, Matthew Broussard? Do we have a future? For the longest time, I was okay with being a teacher and taking care of Tiffany. It was a manageable existence, enough for me. But suddenly, the possibility of being in love and someone loving me seemed within my reach.

Chapter Twenty-one
The Renaissance Man

The litmus test of accepting Matt's Facebook request gave him the courage to send his manuscript in an email, all 44,000 words of it. He embedded a little note about entering it into a literary contest in New Orleans with a due date of April 10. I was afraid to open the attachment, afraid he was a bad writer, afraid the manuscript was about sexually deviant zombies roaming the French Quarter, afraid he would not be what I saw New Year's Eve.

I replied that I could read the manuscript in a month, but no line editing. Too much work. It would be an overall review of the manuscript's strengths and weaknesses.

After hitting send, I became a social media voyeur.

The first clues to this Renaissance man was his Facebook page. He had a list of his favorite books posted: James Joyce's *Ulysses*, Hemingway's *The Old Man and the Sea*, and Steinbeck's *East of Eden*. What could I deduct from this psychological profile? Smart and sensitive? The next clue was the emblem of the Navy SEALs on his page. *He didn't tell me he was a SEAL. A SEAL wounded in combat!* Maybe he was a real man, a man fully fleshed, fully thinking and feeling. I poured myself a glass of wine and studied his pictures on Facebook. I was a thoroughly modern woman—my need to know exceeded any rights to privacy for him.

The pictures revealed a man who had invested his life in the military. Portraits of soldiers with their arms draped across each other's shoulders, beautiful young men carrying M4s, with backdrops of bombed streets and shelled buildings. Men in bars. Men on boats. It was an elite brotherhood that took them to the Persian Gulf, the Kuwaiti coast, Kandur, Mosul, Damascus, Baghdad . . . the Gulf War became the War on Terror, and on, and on, and on. This was the SEAL life with very little room, time, or emotion for anyone or anything else. For a woman to consider a life with such a man, she would need the strength to lasso a Category Five hurricane.

Were these the women on Matt's Facebook page? Portraits of thin, long-haired women, who chose every article of clothing they wore by how well the fabric accentuated every curve of their bodies. These women were as self-assured in their sexuality, as the men were in their masculinity. Girlfriends? Wives? Just looking at them made me feel like a twelve-year-old girl in a training bra.

My last bit of investigation on the World Wide Web concluded with the Travis County Sheriff Department's Registered Sexual Offenders home page. I typed the name in the search engine and *voilà!* Matt Broussard was not a sexual predator with a record.

Friday morning rolled around after a week of grading, teaching, eating, and sleeping. Tiffany acknowledged the $500 check I sent her with a text. I didn't expect more than that. If I did, I was setting myself up for disappointment. I only wanted to know what the doctor said or whoever would be providing her with an examination at the clinic. If this baby were born with any birth defects or complications, I would carry that burden. Tiffany asked, but I supplied the drug. Adderall. Guilty for the rest of my life!

The tortuous "what ifs" taunted me. Despite every medical website I researched, despite the silent will to make the words appear differently on the page, there was no variation in the effects the drug had on women and their unborn children. Let me see, the words I tortured myself with: highly addictive, strokes, seizures, heart attacks. Adderall was defined as a Category C drug for pregnant women, take only if the benefits outweigh the risk. Typical of most pharmaceutical warnings, there were benefits as well as a laundry list of "may affect your heart, lung, kidney, bladder, sex drive, memory. . . ."

Adderall caused birth defects and miscarriages in rodents. Other studies with mice showed the drug to cause problems with brain chemicals, resulting in long term learning and memory problems. *GUILTY. GUILTY. GUILTY.*

So, when Kelly caught me standing in front of my classroom door that Friday morning, waiting for the first block of students to appear, it was the opportune moment for her to convince me Fergal's Irish Pub was a good idea for tonight.

"Is Carl coming?" I took a second to see what she was wearing, anything to take me away from Adderall Land. Her tee shirt was black with white letters, reading ROCK THE KASHBAH. The skirt was of Middle Eastern tribal pattern in black and white. The outfit was complete with a pair of black Doc Martens. She never failed to entertain me with her wardrobe.

"Of course, he is."

"Count me in. I need to get out of my cage for a while. Should I ask Leona?"

"Sure. She might love it."

"A Hungarian in an Irish Pub?"

"Sounds like the punchline of a joke."

The bell rang and we retired into our individual classrooms. At lunch, I called and invited Leona.

"What should I wear?"

"Something casual. It's just a beer and wing place."

"I've never heard of such a place. Perhaps some simple pants and a sweater."

"That will work, Leona. Look. Got to go. I'm on cafeteria duty. I'll pick you up about six, so we can get the happy hour specials."

"Must we? Let's think quality, not quantity, Karen."

"Leona, got to go. My boss is giving me the stink eye."

Principal Kenny walked toward me, shaking his finger. Yes, twenty-first century Kenny was shaking his finger at me.

"Ms. Anders, there's zero tolerance for cell phone use."

"Please, Kenny, we're on a first name basis here. If you want to chastise me, at least call me by my first name."

"You know, Karen, you're your own worst enemy."

"That's what I hear. The cell phone, well, consider it gone. You won't have to keep it in your desk until the end of the day."

"Whatever. Just do your job."

And just like that, he magically disappeared into the abyss of a large urban high school vortex. Maybe I shouldn't have invited Leona. Kenny's exchange might have been an omen for the night. For some reason, everyone felt the need to chastise me. Nothing was going to turn out right for this girl-woman.

"I have something for you, Karen." Leona, red sweater, black pants and a sassy little leopard-print scarf around her neck, handed me a prescription bottle. I read the label.

"Wellbutrin? Antidepressant, right? Leona, don't beat around the bush here. What are you trying to tell me, besides I'm a slob and drink too much?"

"You don't think I recognize you in myself. I drank out of loneliness for years. This will help with the depression and reduce the cravings for alcohol."

"This is a fine start to the evening. Why don't I just check myself into rehab before going to the pub?"

"Don't be overdramatic. See if it helps. If it does, see your doctor for another prescription." She folded her hands across her purse resting on her thigh. I put the Jeep in reverse, backed out of the driveway, and headed toward Fergal's.

Carl and Kelly had secured a table for us near the bar. A pile of chicken bones were stacked in front of Carl, while two-for-one draft mugs encircled Kelly.

"Hi, Gorgeous," Kelly greeted Leona with a warm embrace. I sat next to Carl. I was mad at Leona. Mad at her presumptuous attitude. Damn Europeans. They're so smug in their directness, cleverly disguised as well-meaning friends. I had enough of her. The doilies. The coffee cakes. I'm fifty years old; I don't need a mother. She hurt my feelings, and she did it so casually. My drinking was not her problem. I was still working a sixty-hour week, when I included lesson plans and grading. I cleaned my own house. I did a lot, a lot for a presumed woman with a drinking problem.

"How you doing, Karen? Didn't see much of you this week?" Carl asked. Now, Carl was a real friend.

"Great. Let me get us a beer; that waitress is taking too long. Kelly, looks like you're doing okay. Leona, glass of wine?"

I could be civil, even when insulted.

"Yes, a nice Spätburgunder."

"This is an Irish pub, Leona. No German wines here."

"Rosé, please."

It was all I could do to keep from rolling my eyes at her. I placed the order at the bar, watching the working stiffs shuffle through the front door.

"Is that your husband?"

I turned to see if she was talking to me or someone else. She was all legs and black hair, late forties, standing at the bar to my right.

"Are you talking to me?"

"Yes, I saw you get up from the table with all the women and the one guy."

"Oh, we're just friends."

"Really. He's cute. He got here about an hour before you did. I've been trying to make eye contact, but he must be distracted by eating. That's a serious pile of chicken bones in front of him."

Who was this woman? She ordered a vodka tonic when the bartender approached her. I waited for the bartender to walk away before continuing our conversation. It just struck me as odd. A woman attracted to Carl. He had always been the science teacher to me. A good friend. I never thought of him as attractive. But he was, looking at him now, across the pub. Sandy brown hair, graying at the temples, a slim body, a few inches over six feet; Carl was an attractive man.

"Why don't you introduce us?" She took a sip of her drink waiting for me to respond.

"Yeah, sure. His name is Carl. I'm Karen. We work together. Let me get my drink order in and we'll go over together."

"Thanks, Karen. Nice to meet you. I'm Brenda. I sell insurance here in the Village."

By the time I got the drinks, she had finished hers and ordered another. Maybe this wasn't a good idea, after all. This was just going to be a bad night. I felt it from the time I picked up Leona and her eyebrow.

"Hey, I want y'all to meet Brenda."

I could tell by the look of shock in Leona's and Kelly's eyes, they hated Brenda's guts before she even sat down. What was I supposed to do? The woman asked a simple question. This is a public place. She can do what she wants.

Brenda took my seat next to Carl. Every word she spoke was emphasized with a pat on Carl's thigh. He liked the attention; in fact, he lapped it up like a starving man. I couldn't tell if he was drunk. I stopped counting the mugs. I'm sure he was like me in many respects. He buried his desires in his work and his bottle. It was rare when he got a little attention. I shouldn't make too much of it.

"There's no band tonight, but there's a jukebox. Dance with me, Carl." She grabbed his hand and led him to the jukebox in the corner. Belly rubbing music filled the pub, as Carl and Brenda took center stage on the little parquet dance floor. How could things get any weirder? Carl couldn't dance and it was obvious he couldn't drink either as he lunged himself over Brenda's small frame, occasionally swaying too far to the left. Brenda uprighted him with a little bump and grind from her right hip as the boom-chick-boom played on.

In a few minutes, a love affair erupted in Fergal's Irish Pub between two strangers. I guess that's what people thought about me and Matt that night. No one cared at the Broken Spoke. But I cared about Carl. Was this woman for real? Or was I jealous watching the possibilities between a man and a woman in the neon glow of a Guinness advertising sign?

The love birds sauntered back to the table. Brenda chirped,

"Patrón shots for all. My treat!" She jumped from the table and headed for the bar.

"I am not drinking Patrón, and I don't think any of you driving a car tonight should either," Leona proclaimed with pursed lips. "I want to be taken home. Who is this atrocious woman? Carl, she is no good. No good. Karen, take me home. I won't be a party to this."

"Sorry you're offended, Leona. She's just a woman who doesn't want to drink alone. Don't go home. I'm sure Kelly would be more than happy to drink your shot," Carl offered.

"It's late. I want to go home."

"Look, everyone. I'll take care of this." I finished my drink and made a bee line for Brenda and the bar. The bartender was placing the five shots of tequila on a tray for her. I picked up mine and drank it at the bar.

"You're too much, Karen," Brenda laughed. "I love your friends, especially Carl."

"No, you don't."

"What?"

"You don't love my friends, and you sure don't love Carl."

"Come on. I'm just having some fun here."

"Not at my expense, my friends', or especially Carl's. In fact, you're going home, right now." I grabbed her by the elbow and escorted her to the front door. Lucky for me, she was drunk enough to be as malleable as play-dough. She might have thought I was leading her to the jukebox to play her favorite song. I opened the front door for her.

"Good night, Brenda. Don't come back in here. Carl and I have known players like you all our lives. It takes us a long time to get over people like you. You're not going to ruin our night." I gave her a gentle nudge to push her through the door frame, and the door closed on her open mouth.

I went back to the bar and paid for the drinks.

"Here," I said placing the shot glasses in front of Carl, Kelly, and Leona. I put Brenda's intended drink in front of my empty chair.

"What happened to Brenda? I thought I saw her leave," Carl asked, looking at me.

"Yeah, she got a text from her husband. She had to go home."

Carl stared at me a long time then he took his drink in one gulp.

"How am I going to get home with you drinking like this?" Leona questioned.

I dug in my purse, felt the prescription bottle of Wellbutrin, then my car keys. I placed the keys in front of Leona.

"Congratulations. You're the DD tonight!"

The last thing I saw before my head hit the pillow was a Facebook notification on my cell. It was a private message from Matt. And just like that my head cleared, my heart swelled, as I read, "When can I come to Houston and take you to dinner?"

Sticky note to self: start a zero-carb diet immediately.

Chapter Twenty-two
Dinner for Two, Please

Dos Arbolitos Mexican Cantina balanced itself against the muddy banks of Buffalo Bayou and a once-white aluminum siding apartment complex. The restaurant's signature dish was the El Jefe Margarita, a satisfying mix of fresh lime juice, agave nectar and tequila, served with the tiniest chips of ice and a salted rim. It was the cure-all for the lonely, anxious, and defeated.

I could not tolerate the unspoken expectations of a romantic dinner at a five-star restaurant on Valentine's night. It was the first time I would see Matt, since our New Year's Eve encounter. We agreed to meet at the restaurant. If things got out of hand, Uber was a text away.

Leona insisted on dressing me. It was a hard-fought compromise. I agreed to a gorgeous set of rubies her husband bought her in Thailand. The simple gold chain and ruby heart pendant with matching earrings and bracelet were beautiful against the black dress I wore. It was still a Houston winter, no snow, but a brisk low forties at night. I wore black tights and a wool black shawl. Simple but elegant. The only thing that could throw the entire ensemble off was my mouth; my mouth under the influence of tequila.

I arrived early and went straight to the bathroom. I smiled at myself in the mirror, pushed my hair around to create a carefree, tousled look and reapplied my lipstick. *This is as good as it gets for anyone over fifty.* I frowned at myself in the mirror and walked out. Matt was talking to the hostess near the register and a giant glass jar of Chiclets.

I tapped him on the shoulder.

"Karen, hey, you look great." He kissed my check and hugged me. "Are you okay with this place? It's not very fancy."

"It's perfect. The food's excellent. Besides, no one will rush us here. It's very low key."

"Okay. Good. The traffic was nuts getting here. Let's have a drink and talk."

The waitress sat us in a booth covered with red vinyl. Above the table was a painting of a Mexican peasant woman in a loose fitting white blouse and a voluptuous neckline. People say they hate the predictable, I crave it. It gives me a lot of comfort to look at the same trite artwork for forty years.

I looked at him as he studied the menu. The chocolate brown eyes, the crooked bottom teeth that showed when he spoke, the dark hair on his arms, his set jawline . . . He was an attractive man in his white button down shirt and expensive jeans. *Get a hold of yourself, Karen. You just got here.* He looked up at me and smiled.

"El Jefe Margarita?"

"*Sí,*" I replied to the waitress, dressed in a Houston Rockets tee shirt and a black pair of yoga pants.

"Want an appetizer?"

"You'd like the snake bites, Matt. It's roasted jalapenos wrapped in bacon."

"Do you smoke cigars and drive fast, too?"

"Only on special occasions," I laughed.

"You know I want to talk about my manuscript. I assumed you've read all of it. Maybe I should wait for my drink before I ask your opinion."

"Actually, I have a few questions about the manuscript." I dug into my purse and found the notes I'd been taking on *Family Tradition*.

"Go ahead. You first. Just be gentle with me. I do have an ego."

I gave him a smile for reassurance. "Are you sure about the title? I mean, it is a song. I think Hank Williams, Jr. put it out a while back, so you might want to research the intellectual property for using the title. Could bite you."

"I did take the title from the song. Remember, I'm writing Southern Grit, trailer parks and the living and loving of the folks who inhabit them."

"Okay. Anyway, it's a fast read. And yes, I did read all of it. It's very entertaining. But why do all the women in the book have to look like underwear models? I mean, how realistic is that to your genre?"

"The women in the book are described that way because men like underwear models."

"Right." *We should have waited until we finished the first round before starting this conversation.* "I thought you had a real eye for description. Lots of imagery describing the small town and the people who lived there. Did you use to live in South Louisiana?"

"Morgan City. My first wife was the Shrimp and Petroleum Queen, if that tells you anything about the town. It's where the Gulf of Mexico meets the Atchafalaya River. I took a lot of my childhood memories and planted them in the book. The South has always been a love-hate thing for me. All that class hierarchy and tradition. It'll choke the life out of you."

"You feel that way about Texas?"

"Texas is different. Texas is wild, independent. It's still got the pioneer mentality, well, maybe not the suburbs surrounding the urban areas. You might as well be in California or Florida suburbs, same stores, same houses, same cars, same people."

The waitress delivered two El Jefes and four snake bites resting on a chipped coffee cup saucer. *This should take the edge off the manuscript review. I knew he wouldn't like what I had to say. Oh, well.*

"To my Valentine." Matt clinked his margarita glass against mine. I smiled and took a generous gulp.

"One more toast. To your book and success as a writer." *A toast and a bone, only a male ego would appreciate this.*

I got what I wanted. He beamed at me from across the table.

"I'm entering it in the novella category for the Crescent City Literary Competition."

"Not familiar with that."

"It's an annual writing competition in New Orleans, followed by a week of overeating and overdrinking. All jokes aside, it is a serious event that pays respect to the great Southern writers, such as Faulkner. April 1 is the deadline to enter. The manuscript is my thesis for the MFA program and my ticket to New Orleans, if I'm lucky."

"That's great. As an English teacher, I'm afraid I don't know the contemporary book world. But I certainly know Faulkner. I hated his work as a kid. Just too hard to read, but as an adult reader, he nails the Deep South angst."

"Now you know why I'm entering the contest with the Southern Grit manuscript."

He took a long sip from his El Jefe and looked at me.

"Why don't you come with me, Karen? The event is in July, so you won't have to worry about your job and taking off."

"I haven't been to New Orleans in years. You know, I'd love it, Matt." One margarita down and suddenly, the world had become a very manageable place. Matt looked at the empty glass in front of me.

"Let's have another drink and order. I hate to rush, but I really haven't eaten much today."

"I've had about everything on the menu. The chili rellenos are excellent; the red sauce has some heat, but it's delicious. Of course, you never can go wrong with steak fajitas. The tortillas are made here. Probably got some old man chained to a table of white flour and lard, spitting them out night and day."

Matt laughed and smiled at me. "What will you have?"

"Chili rellenos."

He turned around and motioned for our waitress. The evening melted into chili peppers, onions, refried beans, margaritas and a man and woman tittering on the possibilities of romance. But back in my mind, back in the comfort zone of I like predictability, no surprises, no trapped doors, I stopped drinking and asked for sopapillas and a cup of coffee. The look Matt gave me when I began drinking coffee was much like my question about the underwear models in his manuscript.

"Where am I staying tonight, Karen?"

I put my coffee cup down and looked at him. "Where do you want to stay?"

"With you."

"I'm not ready for that, Matt. Believe me, I've thought about it since I first met you in Austin. I don't want to mess things up by rushing into something. I know we're not kids. All the more reason to think before I act. I hardly know you."

"What's to know? You've read my manuscript. Scratch just a little beneath the fiction and you read me."

"I know that. That's why I don't want to rush. It's been a long time since I've met an attractive man, who is also really smart."

"It's the same for me, Karen. You're funny. You're real. You're beautiful."

"Now, that's the El Jefe talking!"

"Take your compliment, Karen. Take it as a woman, not the clown you hide behind."

I didn't say anything else for a while. I didn't know if I had been insulted.

"Hey, what else do you want to know?" He reached for my hand across the table.

"Have you been married before?"

"Is that a trick question?"

"No. I'm divorced. I'm also the adoptive mother of, *well, how do I describe Tiffany? College dropout, pregnant and living with a loser?* I have a daughter in Austin, at UT. She's struggling with some things right now that have me very distracted. I teach high school; sometimes it's magical, sometimes I need a whip and a chair to get through it. I'm not big on the dating scene. I had a few dates; the last one was a dinner date. The creep actually asked me to feed him and picked up my hand holding a fork and moved it to his mouth. Just weird, sad and all the above. You're the first guy I've met in a long time I wanted to know better."

"Okay, Karen. This doesn't have to be a confession scene, but I've been married three times, but only had two wives."

"What?"

"I married the same woman twice. One great night does not a marriage make."

I laughed and squeezed his hand. "Kids?"

"The first wife wanted them; I was never home. The second one, the one I married twice, was too vain to have kids. Worked out for the best, don't you think?"

"Matt, let's end the night here. I've loved every minute. Come by tomorrow morning at nine for breakfast. I don't live far from here. You'll love my house; it's an old pier and beam, mission style. I'll text you directions when I get home."

"So tonight ends just like that."

"Yeah, just like that, but we pick up again tomorrow morning."

"Okay, but I'm not happy about it. Sorry, I'm just being a guy." He motioned for the check.

The night ended in front of the hand-painted Dos Arbolitos sign. I was the first one to pull away from the kiss. His mouth was deliciously salty from the margaritas. I hugged him quickly and walked away, all the while wondering if he was staring at my butt, sculpted by a very expensive panty girdle.

Chapter Twenty-three
The Beginning of Something Beautiful

I set the alarm for 6:00 a.m. the night before and jumped out of bed on the first BEEP from my Eighties digital clock radio. That thirty-five-year-old alarm clock was one of the few things still working in my world. I hadn't a minute to spare between cleaning the house, cooking breakfast, and doing my face and hair. I had to give Matt the impression this is how I rolled every Sunday morning of my life. Perfect house, best cook, adorable pets, and pretty woman, today and every day of the year. The first call was to Leona. I knew she'd be up baking bread or making doilies.

"Morning, neighbor. I've got another favor to ask you today."

"Karen, what are you doing up at this hour on a Sunday? You usually don't open the living room curtains until after noon. Did something happen with that man you were meeting for dinner?"

"It was a nice evening, but an early one. I've invited him over for breakfast this morning, and I'm wondering if you have an extra coffee cake I can borrow."

"To borrow? This is ridiculous, Karen! What is going on?"

"Please don't make me beg, Leona, because you know I will. He's coming over for breakfast at nine. I want to impress him and I don't think frozen waffles are going to do it. Help me out."

"Karen, this man may come to expect every morning to be like this, if your friendship grows. You best not lie. Be yourself."

"Leona. Do this for me."

"I suppose, well, let me see what I have in the cupboard, poppy seed, walnuts, I will do a nice Kalacs for you."

"What do I serve with it? Is it sweet? What?"

"It is a Hungarian cinnamon swirl bread. Fresh coffee and juice would be lovely. Do you have a few nice dishes to serve it on?"

"Of course, I do."

"How am I to know, Karen? You've not once had me for dinner, not even an informal lunch."

"Leona, let me take care of today, then I'll take care of you. Maybe dinner and a movie this coming week. All right?"

"Yes. I will have the Kalacs before he arrives. Do you have decent table linens?

I ignored that question. She was going to do what she wanted to do, regardless of whether I had Irish linen and gold rim serving plates. Her stuff, her ideas, her *everything* would always be better, because I was an American girl-woman. But I was desperate to impress a man I hardly knew, and Leona was the woman to take me to the next level of smoke and mirrors in the dating game.

"Appreciate your help, Leona." I hung up, plugged in the curling iron and plucked my eyebrows while it heated. Sticky note to self: make a tweezing appointment for Leona and her eyebrow. It might give her a whole new view of the world.

Matt knocked at the door at nine o'clock. Before I opened it, I had a quick mental test straight out of the Mystery Date board game. Would I open the door to the blond haired, blue eyed man in a white sport jacket holding a bouquet of flowers or would it be the beach bum with a tattered Mexican hat on his head and a can of beer in his hand? Only time would tell. I took a deep breath and opened the door. Behind the white door at 213 White Oak stood a dark haired, dark eyed man in a pair of khaki shorts and a black tee shirt. How refreshing to see a plain tee shirt, without political slogans or free advertising for the designer who made the shirt! In his hand was a bottle of champagne. He kissed me on the cheek, walked through the threshold and into my heart. Just like that.

I set a cozy nook for us in the kitchen with candles, Kalacs, coffee, cantaloupe and mimosas. Max sat on my feet underneath the table. Poncho did a brief inspection of Matt, circling the chair Matt sat in, then weaved his tail around Matt's leg. Matt kept staring at Poncho with an unspoken question on his lips.

"Matt, did you want to ask me if I have thirty cats living in my bedroom?" He started laughing. "No, Max and Poncho are it for pets; they're the only ones."

"Max is like a fine old gentleman," he scratched behind Max's ear, touching my leg when he did. "I see he is very protective of you. But cats? Cats love cats, that's it. I guess I didn't grow up with them, so they're strange animals to me."

"No, you're right about Poncho. Poncho loves Poncho. Max and I exist for his entertainment. Well, Max exists for processed cheese slices wrapped in cellophane. But Poncho is a completely different story. If I'm a minute late putting his food out, he's circling me, screaming meow until I do his bidding. Cats are the visual of the human super ego. Dogs represent human enlightenment, that's Maslow's hierarchy of self-actualization."

"What?" He laughed, grabbing my hand on the table and squeezing it.

"Sorry, that was the champagne talking. But don't you think it's true?"

"I do, Karen." He offered me a warm smile. "Hey, you were right about your house. It's a fine craftsman. Beautiful heart of pine floors. My folks' house was like this in Morgan City. Bad thing was the wind blew through those old windows in the winter. Hot as hell in the summer."

"Most of the floors are original. I put tile in the bathroom. It's a lot of work keeping her up, labor of love. You don't own an old house, rather it owns you. Best thing I got from a bad marriage."

"Does your daughter come home to this house in the summer or stay in Austin?"

"No, well, I don't know what she'll do this summer. I'm her adoptive mother, oh, I think I told you that already. Tiffany's my brother's child. When he died unexpectedly, I adopted her. Anyway, that's the short version of the story." With that, I stood up. No more drinking and no more digging up bones from the past. Not on a Sunday.

"I shouldn't have asked. It's none of my business."

"There's just a lot going on with Tiffany right now. But, she's my world. I've raised her as a single working mom, with all the good and bad that comes with that. Some stuff I was great at; others, well, I couldn't be mom and dad rolled into one, no matter how hard I tried. She's beautiful and smart. She's my Hope Diamond."

He stood up from the table and hugged me.

"You're beautiful and smart."

How could I not laugh out loud? The corny line, the hopeless game between a man and a woman, and the residual effects of champagne made it all seem so ridiculous. I turned around and faced him.

"I'm all over the place this morning, Matt. Let's have a bite to eat and talk about your manuscript."

He obeyed me and sat down in front of Leona's plate of Kalacs. He took his frustration out on a bite of buttery, cinnamon bread.

"Wow, you bake this?"

I wanted to lie. It was on the tip of my tongue to take credit for sixty-odd years of Hungarian pastry mastery. The only thing that stopped me was the probability he would ask me to produce something spectacular in the kitchen, and I wouldn't have time to bully Leona into doing it.

"My neighbor made these. She's Hungarian. It's a specialty bread, Kalacs."

"My compliments to her. Delicious."

"Yes, Leona is something else. I'm sure you'll meet her. She does a lot for me. Took care of Max and Poncho the weekend I met you."

"Good woman." He picked up another pastry and ate it.

"Your manuscript. I just did a quick read. If you're comfortable, I can read for editing. Maybe highlight some things that need polishing then you can decide whether to change it or keep it as is. Want to give you your best shot at this contest."

"Appreciate it, Karen," he offered between bites.

Oh, for Pete's sake, the morning is quickly becoming Leona and the Kalacs.

"I'll look up this contest online, start making some travel plans. It's been a long time since I've been in New Orleans."

He nodded at me between bites.

"You know the only New Orleans I know is as an undergrad on Bourbon Street in the Eighties. I'm sure it's changed."

He wasn't coming up for air with the Kalacs. Leona had cast her spell.

We spent the next hour chatting about writing and New Orleans. Before I walked Matt to the front door, I placed two pastries in a Ziploc bag and handed it to him.

"Thanks, Karen. It's been a great morning. Better get out of here, the Sunday traffic will be intense getting back to Austin. Call you tonight." He kissed me on the cheek and was gone. I stood in the driveway watching him back out. I glanced over at Leona's. She was standing in front of her bay window, curtains parted, watching the scene unfold. I waved at the bay window.

If I hurried, I'd make it to 11:30 Mass at St. Thérèse. I don't know if I was feeling thankful, religious, or even optimistic. But I felt something I hadn't felt in a long time. I felt I could sit among the families in that church. Me, a divorced, middle-aged woman, sitting by women with their grandchildren in their lap, with their life partners kissing them during the sign of peace, with their perfectly normal, healthy families surrounding them, kneeling with them after receiving Communion. I could sit with them and not feel the singular existence I lived next to their enormity of life, eating at my heart like a leper at the gate.

This Sunday my loneliness and feelings of failure as a former wife and adoptive parent would not send me running from the hidden, back pew before the Mass had ended. This Sunday I belonged to something bigger than myself.

Chapter Twenty-four
March Menagerie

The wind and cold rain of early March whipped and pelted the students and me, as we ran from the open courtyard near the cafeteria entrance to the Social Sciences Building for third block classes. The last class of the day. Nobody wanted it, but here we were, a collective mass arriving at the same place at the same time, hoping somehow, we'd hear something different.

"How much longer 'til Spring Break?" asked Raul Sanchez, the last one to enter the door, as the tardy bell was ringing.

"It begins with the Ides of March," Brandon Jacobs answered from the front row, knowing full well Raul didn't know the date for the Ides of March, much less what it meant.

"It begins the week before Easter, around March 15," I said, while taking roll, bobbing my head from the attendance book to the face of a student.

"Why's it called the Ides of March?" Raul asked.

"It's a day to watch your back," Brandon laughed.

"Right, man, like some gangster died on that day," offered Raul.

"Exactly." Brandon laughed into his unopened backpack on his desk.

Just as I was about to offer Raul a more literary interpretation, I heard the cell phone in my purse buzz. I made a mental note to check it after class.

"The Ides of March is a date noted for the assassination

of Julius Caesar and a transition from the Roman Empire to the Roman Republic." Immediately after saying it, I realized I was guilty of the same thing Brandon was. Rhetoric, rhetoric, rhetoric. He who knows wins, and he who doesn't, falls further and further down the line.

"Class, let's take a look at the T.S. Eliot poem on page 389. If you forgot your book, be sneaky and borrow from the class set at the back of the room. Just don't let me see you. You know how I get. Let's review 'The Love Song of J. Alfred Prufrock.' Brandon, please read the first stanza for us."

He gave me a dirty look but began reading. When he began the second stanza with a British accent, I took over.

"There's so much in every word of this poem. What is Eliot telling us? The line about disturbing the universe . . ."

Caitlyn Levin, a seventeen-year-old smoldering package of teenage angst and post-punk rocker with purple hair, interrupted me.

"Ms. Anders, did this poet commit suicide? This is one lonely, neurotic man, afraid of the world he lives in and everyone in it. He's terrified to make a decision."

"Caitlyn, that's a great understanding of Prufrock, but the poet, Eliot, died of emphysema. Let's look at that line again, 'For decisions and revisions . . .'"

"Exactly," Caitlyn interrupted, again. "The man is catatonic in the modern world, paralyzed by what can happen at any minute."

Oh, my dear Caitlyn, keep your edge; that self-confidence marked by the kohl black eyeliner coating your eyelids and the jeans worn like denim skin; don't ever become middle-aged, or you'll be just like Prufrock and me, measuring our lives with coffee spoons.

My afternoon melted into the raw emotion of the teenage view of the world; a place where poets and musicians are Gods, and the banal and trite are fodder for those under the age of twenty.

Raul did not take part in the conversation, but chose to sleep behind his textbook propped up on his desk. But even Raul would have appreciated Caitlyn's comment; even Raul was an original and fearless in the eyes of phonies.

True to his nature, he was the last student to leave when the dismissal bell sounded, rising from his afternoon nap with a luxurious stretch and yawn.

"Have a good day, Mr. Sanchez." I smiled at him.

"Hey man, you too, Miss Anders. Peace."

I wondered if he would always be the last to arrive and the last to leave. With that passing thought, I picked up my cell phone. There was a text from Tiffany.

"Saw Doc this morning. Baby OKAY ❤" This cryptic message was followed by a glossy red heart emoticon.

"Great! Time to plan a baby shower," I texted. I waited for her to respond while clearing my desk and packing my satchel with a stack of ungraded essays. Wine and essays tonight. Was there any other way?

"Call you tonight," she texted back.

Tiffany had a lot she wanted to talk about; I interpreted it as a good sign. Please don't let it be some weird Adderall mishap. Please. Let this just be a happy, normal little conversation about baby showers, storks and pastel mints. If I were truly lucky, I'd get a positive call from her, a sexy call from Matt, with wine and essays in between.

"How was your day?" Kelly asked, sticking her head into the open classroom door.

"Eliot and Sanchez saved it. How about yours?"

"Good. Got a date tonight!" She proclaimed it as it she had just won the lottery.

"Really. Who's the guy?"

"My neighbor, the engineer."

"No, not the one who wears Hawaiian shirts year-round."

"Yep, that one." Kelly walked in and sat at one of the student desks near mine. She was wearing an orange-and-blue stripped knit dress with red felt boots. The look was more impish than elfish on her.

"Well, how did this start?"

"I was taking out the garbage last Sunday and saw him in his front yard, doing the same thing. He was back from his trip to Puerto Rico, visiting some Russian woman and her kid."

"Now, that doesn't sound right. A Russian woman and her kid?"

"Oh yeah, he's been seeing her since I met him several years ago. He brings her negligees and her daughter, Barbies. Perfect union, wouldn't you say?"

"No," I laughed. "There may be something wrong with him if his only date is a woman desperate for citizenship."

"Oh, you know the old engineer joke. Best form of birth control is an engineer's personality."

"So, you're going out with him?"

"Well, after our little chat by the side of the road, we learned a lot about each other. Namely, we're about the same age; he loves Dino's pizza like me, and he's promised to change the brakes on the Volkswagen. He's a genius. What more could I ask for?"

"Kelly, you've come a long way from hitting on frat daddies half your age. I'm proud of you. But are you attracted to him? I mean, what about the kiss goodnight thing?"

"The kiss goodnight thing? I've never had a problem with that. Physical attraction is fleeting, but food and a new brake job, like money in the bank."

She followed me to the classroom door, where I reached back in and turned out the light on another day, another chance to embed the words of a poet, to smile at adolescent wonderment, and to love my friend for who she was.

Chapter Twenty-Five
Little, Lost Lamb

Thursday evening loomed across the skyline of Houston, grey with rain and pollution. Hopefully, the weekend would bring sunnier weather; at least a day I could walk Max beyond the boundaries of Leona's yard. Saturday afternoon was her appointment, or rather her eyebrow's appointment, for grooming and a pedi/mani. She deserved it. She had been a good friend to me, and despite the occasional insult of referring to me as a girl-woman, I had come to love her. Leona was a mother-figure to me, which was pathetic considering I still needed mothering at fifty. I was about to call Leona and remind her of our day of beauty, when I got a text from Tiffany.

"Can you talk?"

"Calling now."

I sat on the couch with a glass of wine between my legs, Max at my feet, and my cell phone in my hand.

"So, you had good news from the doc. That's terrific, baby. How you feeling?"

"Not so good. Just had a big fight with Jared."

"What's going on?"

"He thinks he's too young to be a dad."

"Oh, really. Little too late for that."

"Stop it, Karen. I don't need a petty argument. I'm having a baby and no one cares."

"I do."

The phone was silent in my hand. I could hear her crying.

"Tiffany, where are you?"

"I'm home. At the apartment."

"Let me come get you. Right now."

"I thought he loved me."

"I don't think it's about that. He can't handle the pressure. You're loveable. Let me love you and take care of you and your baby. Come home."

"What about school? I got two classes this semester. Two classes and I can't even do that. I've screwed up my entire life in a matter of months."

"You can go to school here."

Silence.

"Tiffany, walk away now. Walk away from this guy and that horrible job. I love you and I will love your baby. We'll be a family. I will be there for you."

"What? We're going to be a family? With a baby and no father?"

"It's the brave new world, whether we like it or not, most kids don't have fathers living with them."

"I wanted more than this. I wanted my life to be different than yours. A single woman raising a kid. I got sucked right back into that world."

"Oh, come on. It's not so bad. We've had some good times. You're not letting yourself remember the good stuff."

"Hey, he's back. I'll talk later."

Just like that she was gone and I was left to think of her in that rat-trap apartment covered in mildew and reeking of Jared. I had to sit 160 miles away and think of him in the same room with her.

I drained my wine glass. I wasn't waiting for the boy to call me; I was calling the boy.

"Hey, thought I'd check up on you."

"Did you, now?" Matt laughed good naturally and the visual in my head of the nightmare in apartment 216 was replaced by the image of Matt's warm smile and chocolate-brown eyes.

"How's the writing going?"

"I'm in the middle of creating a great chapter with my

femme fatale in an Ellie Mae Clampett dress, pointing an M-16 at her untrue lover."

"What?" I laughed. "Oh, that's right, the genre is Southern Grit. Perfect."

"Not only that but the actress who portrayed Ellie Mae Clampett, Donna Douglass in the *Beverley Hillbillies* series is from Pride, Louisiana."

"Never heard of Pride, Louisiana."

"No, but the judges of the writing contest in the great state of Louisiana haven't forgotten a successful native daughter."

"You don't miss a trick."

"Can't afford to."

"It's good to hear your voice, Matt." With that line, I stepped a little deeper into the unchartered territory of does he like me as much as I like him.

"What's wrong? You're not this affectionate with me. I've been the pursuer; now, you're switching roles. Makes me nervous," Matt laughed.

"Well, remember Tiffany? It's all coming to a head. She's pregnant; I hate her loser boyfriend, and I can't stand the thought of her living with him."

"She's in Austin, right? Give me the address. I can go over there now, kick that punk's butt and bring your daughter home to Houston by midnight."

"Whoa, cowboy, slow down here. I thought you were the sensitive writer type."

"Baby, I'm the man to get the job done." I had a visual of him wrestling alligators as a teenager.

"I don't think the shotgun approach is going to work. Tiffany's smart and independent. She's afraid of ending up like me: a single woman raising a child."

"Let's get this over with, Karen."

"No. I'll call her later and offer to move her home. If I force her, she'll move in the opposite direction. She's always been like that."

"Okay. Come to Austin this weekend. Stay with me. I'll help you move her out."

"No, I can't."

"Some time in the near future, Karen, you're going to have to decide where I fit in in all this. You keep giving me mixed messages. I don't even think you know what you want."

"Matt, I want someone else to make all the decisions and worry about the consequences. I want Tiffany home. I want you here. I want a normal life, just like everybody else. Just like a million women all over the world, I want to be loved and needed." My heart stopped when I finished talking. Silence. *Was he hanging up? Maybe he thinks I'm nuts.*

"Just like that Sunday morning breakfast with you, you're all over the place, Maslow's Hierarchy, cats and dogs, quoting poets, hot and cold, sexy, then a matron. But, I'm a man who loves a mystery. You're an enigma, Karen. I want to unravel you."

"I'll come see you in Austin. Just not now."

"Goodnight, Karen. If you change your mind about that punk your daughter's living with, just call."

"Goodnight, Matt."

I turned out the living room lights and got ready for bed. When I lay down, I thought of Tiffany. I prayed for her and her little baby. I turned out the light next to the bed. There in the quiet dark, I thought of Matt. *Please, God, let me dream of dancing with that man.*

Chapter Twenty-six
It's All Relative

Leona's black pants, white blouse and black-and-white polka dot scarf even amused the esthetician at the Bayou Oaks Salon and Day Spa on Gessner. The platinum blonde with zero body fat welcomed her into a black leather recliner under a massive lamp with a twangy, "You sit right here, Mzzz. Supak and make yourself comfy." The skinny blonde quickly turned, flipped the switch on a vat of wax, then grabbed a cloth strip for Leona's eyebrow shaping.

"Let's prepare the area," sang the esthetician. I almost finished the statement with "for landing," but decided Leona would interpret it as sarcasm, rather than humor. It wasn't easy convincing her to come. I preferred not mentioning eyebrow grooming when I first approached her with the idea, referring to Bayou Oaks Salon and Day Spa as a more congenial day of beauty, a gift for a loyal, supportive friend.

As I watched the esthetician coat Leona's eyebrow area with astringent, I couldn't help but notice a fleur-de-lis placed strategically on each back pocket of her jeans. They were outlined in rhinestones. I wondered if she owned a BeDazzler and this was an example of her craftsmanship or if the jeans were specifically purchased because of the rhinestones on the buttocks.

"Do you have a particular shape in mind?" quizzed the esthetician.

Leona's eyes darted to mine, searching for an answer.

"I think my sweet friend would love for you to clean up the natural brow line," I purred. Leona's eyes smiled back at me.

Following the removal of the hairy shapeless animal extended across Leona's forehead, a hand massage and manicure followed. The usually rigid, no-nonsense Leona became a stick of butter under the magic of Bayou Oaks Salon and Day Spa. I sipped the salon's coffee, dutifully noted by the sign above the French press, that the beans were hand-picked, brought from the mountains of the Himalayas by slipper-footed llamas. As I browsed through beauty magazines, I was painfully reminded that my hair, face, body, and clothes were woefully out of shape, date, and style. I took comfort in knowing these beautiful young women in the magazines were probably unloved heroin addicts who were painstakingly airbrushed. Jealousy is a horrible trait and women are evil creatures. This was my disclaimer to my own shortcomings as a woman. At least I was good to the old woman across the street, I told myself, watching her from my cushioned perch. Her eyes were closed and her back actually slouched from its usual broomstick position.

By the time I paid and handed the esthetician a tip, it was four in the afternoon. If we hurried, we'd make happy hour at Dos Arbolitos and two-for-one El Jefe margaritas. Leona was reluctant.

"My treat. Let's just make a day of it, Leona. Live a little."

"Drinking in the middle of the afternoon is not my idea of living a little." Leona brushed the back of her right hand against her new eyebrows as if to block out the realization of where the afternoon would end. "It is very tiresome for me to constantly remind you of what the outcome will be."

"Oh, come on." I backed the car out of Bayou Oaks and headed for Dos Arbolitos. I could almost taste the salt on the rim of my first El Jefe.

Black-and-white Leona ordered an iced tea, without sugar, during Happy Hour. When my first margarita arrived, I saluted her. When the second margarita was delivered, I began telling her about Tiffany. When the third margarita was slid in front of me, I cried in the chips and salsa.

"Must every social event with you begin and end the same way," Leona said, motioning to the lone waitress in a tie-dye maxi with a dingy grey bra strap sliding down her left arm. "Coffee, one black coffee."

"I'm not drinking it, Leona. Miss, don't bring it."

"Bring the coffee," Leona demanded. The waitress strolled away from our table, her flip-flops slapping against the terrazzo tile.

"I need your sympathy. Why can't you be a friend to me?"

"You're exactly right. I'm the one friend who will tell you the truth. Stop feeling sorry for yourself. So, Tiffany's pregnant and you hate her boyfriend. Do something about it."

"I can't kidnap her."

"Of course not. Give her a reason to come home, Karen. She's tired and confused. Be the grown-up to give her a place to rest, instead of carrying on like this. Tiffany is not the first woman in the world to get pregnant by a man who doesn't love her."

"She wanted more for herself. So did I. But you, stoic Leona. You don't know what you want. All you know is what you had." The waitress returned with the coffee. "Bring me another El Jefe. Don't say a damn word, Leona. I'm old enough to drink." The waitress scurried away from the table.

"You're being cruel. But that's how you Americans are. You think you know what life is. You think you know what it's worth. Your people don't get sprinkles on their chocolate donuts, and the world is ending. Try being hungry when there's no food to be had or thirsty and the only water is mingled with blood and dung. Grow up and face what's in front of you instead of drinking and crying. I'll not be a part of this. Next time, bring Kelly and her tramp wardrobe with you. Two grown women acting like children."

"Don't get nuts on me, Leona. We came in here to have a nice time. Oh, that's right, fun is not part of your vocabulary. Yes, Kelly is fun. You're not."

"You're calling a cab for us. Now. I refuse to drive your car, bailing you out one more time." She drained the glass of iced tea in front of her and placed her purse on top of the table.

The waitress returned with the fourth El Jefe. I downed it looking directly at Leona. I returned the glass to the waitress and asked for the check.

At the register, I pulled out my cell phone and sent Uber a message. Serendipity! A driver would be at Dos Arbolitos in fifteen minutes.

"Have a seat." I pointed Leona to a red wrought-iron chair beneath a plastic banana tree in a dark corner near the entrance. She immediately sat down and folded both arms across her chest. I laughed, grabbed a handful of Chiclets from the jar near the register and blew a purple bubble in her direction.

After studying the dust on the plastic banana leaves for a few more minutes, the Uber driver arrived in a late model Dodge Caravan. I chose to sit up front with him. Leona sat on the bench seat in the rear.

"Take us home, we're having too much fun," I sang to the driver, a portly middle-aged man with a Fu Manchu mustache in a faded maroon jogging suit. Between the cup holders and the console, a large print edition Bible lay open to the Book of Revelations.

"Doing some light reading here?"

"Sunday's sermon is on Revelations."

"Are you a preacher?"

"No, ma'am, I'm a deacon for the largest non-denominational church in the USA. Right here in Houston. The House of Love. Westheimer at 59. Use to be the indoor basketball court for the Houston Cougars, back when Clyde Drexler and Hakeem Olajuwon played."

"I remember Phi Slama Jama. Bitter last minute loss to NC State. Don't know your church, though."

"Why don't you visit us tomorrow?" The deacon Uber driver took a sharp left at North Shepherd, sending Leona sliding to the opposite end of the bench seat. "I can pick you and your friend up. No charge."

"Well, I don't think I need to go to Six Flags over Jesus to find God, Deacon."

"No, you don't, ma'am; he's sitting right here next to you, crying his eyes out that you're drunk in the middle of the afternoon."

"I guess you're not expecting a tip." I thought I heard Leona snicker from the back. "Right you are, Deacon. I'm a sinner. You don't need to save me today, but you can drop us off in front of the house, 213 White Oak. There it is. The one with the sagging front porch."

"I didn't mean to offend you, ma'am. I want to help."

"Well here's a tip for you; mind your own damn business and for God's sake, shave that ridiculous thing off your upper lip." I hopped out of the van, leaving behind one flip-flop, and slid down the front curb. After pulling my dress down over my hips, I approached the open car door.

"Deacon, could you hand me my other shoe?"

He silently obeyed. I slammed the door closed and bent down to put on my other shoe. I could see Leona's sensible low-heeled sandals approaching me. I looked up.

"How many more signs from God do you need, Karen?" With that, she stormed across the street to her doily collection.

Chapter Twenty-seven
The Straight and True

I spent a week apologizing and mopping up the mess I created with Leona. Instead of wine for supper, I drank water and ate microwave popcorn. Sobriety and weight-loss was a tough combo, but by Friday my hands stopped shaking in the morning and I could zip my jeans without squeezing my gut.

Leona kept her distance most of the week, but agreed to keep Max and Poncho for the weekend. I decided for each mile of that 160-mile trip to Austin, I was throwing a mental handicap out the window. By the time I arrived at Matt's, I'd no longer be that girl-woman Leona despised.

I didn't want to be that person anymore. The middle-aged, lonely English teacher drinking herself to sleep every night, a coward hiding behind a routine and assumed responsibilities. I would no longer be the parent who communicated with her child through texts. To admit that out loud made me very, very sad. I was that woman.

The night before I left for Austin, I entered a 1,500-word creative essay in the Crescent City Literary Competition. The same contest Matt had entered his novella. I made the deadline by a few days. I didn't know if the essay had a chance. It was more of a literary confession, a stream of consciousness apology for being a drunk and a middle-aged brat with the sobering title, "Drinking Alone."

I left for Austin as soon as the last bell rang at Heights

Central. Avoiding Principal Kenny and his henchmen coaches, I was the first faculty member out of the parking lot. Kelly and I exchanged bus duties with her taking my watch that afternoon. Taking her duty would bring me to school almost two hours before the first block, but Monday morning was a world away. I was living for this weekend.

As Houston became smaller in my rearview mirror, nearly fifty miles out from my neighborhood, I dropped each regret and mistake I'd ever made out the window, counting them by mile-markers. I didn't pray, but I thought about the Mexican woman who sat with me that day in the chapel. I thought about the Uber Deacon. I thought a lot about Leona. It took a long time for a girl-woman to grow up. Maybe, maybe this time, I'll know how to enjoy a man and take my daughter home.

Matt's condo was located on Riverside Drive, east of Congress. The Colorado River was in sight with green space, bike racks, and Austinites being Austinites. This was a town where tee shirts and bumper stickers resounded the inhabitants' view of themselves—Austintatious. They were a living pun! But the more counterculture Austin claimed itself to be, the more mainstream it became. You had to have the right clothes, funk, and smell to live in this city. If you didn't, you stood out like a tourist in Bermuda shorts and a Hawaiian shirt. I admit I wasn't cool. I was a working stiff from Houston. Big deal.

I was nervous when I arrived, so I drove through the area, trying to get my courage up. After twenty minutes of staring at joggers and bench sitters, I drove to the condo entrance, parked in visitor parking, wondering immediately if that was the right thing to do. Tow truck drivers in Austin made a six-figure income towing drunks and the illegally parked. It was a bad day if you happened to be both, which in Austin, might have been the rule instead of the exception.

I stared at numbers on the condo door before knocking. I thought about my hair, breath, weight, underwear, and wrinkles.

These were the checkpoints in dating. Was I dating Matt? What is dating for middle-aged people? I was Prufrock. *Do I dare?*

I gave a sharp, three-count knock to the door. He opened. All smiles. *I'm not going to be able to do this.*

"Come in, come in," he grabbed my suitcase and pulled me in. My first few minutes in his world was a view of a large white leather sectional, white shag rug, with an acrylic painting of a marlin over the sectional. A little matchy-matchy for a guy, but hey, he's ex-military. He's structured.

"I'm putting your things in the loft upstairs," he announced, taking control immediately.

Good. I'm glad that's out of the way.

He returned. Again, all smiles. "Come in the kitchen. I'm making shrimp etouffee, just for you."

I smelled it. An intoxicating mix of olive oil, garlic, onion, bell pepper and shrimp simmering in a rich, dark brew. A little pot of rice sat on the side burner. The table was set and a bottle of white was opened.

"Matt, this is so nice. I had no idea . . ."

"I know. Once you tell people you're ex-military and from South Louisiana, they expect you to eat only fried catfish and grits."

"No, I'd never define you as a stereotype," I laughed. "It's, it's good to be here."

"Good to have you, Karen." He turned around and opened the oven door. "Store bought bread, but it has lots of butter on it." He pulled out a cookie sheet with a French loaf cut in half.

"I promised myself not to talk so much this time. I don't know much about you. South Louisiana. I see on your Facebook page you were a SEAL. Does that make you a Cajun SEAL? Sounds exotic."

"Growing up in Morgan City taught me to be a water man. That town was originally called Tiger Island; a little spit of land between the Atchafalaya River and the Gulf of Mexico. The land meets the water there. The only thing that keeps the town from washing away is a levy system and a twelve-foot steel gate that shuts out the water during hurricanes and the annual flooding of the river in spring." Matt ladled shrimp etouffee over mounds of rice in two bowls and set them on the table.

"Come sit down."

"My mouth has been watering since I walked into the kitchen. Thank you, I will."

"Tiger Island. Morgan City. It had it all. Oil, seafood industry, forestry. But you know there's a handful of people that made a killing off that town's good fortune. The rest of us just went to work in those industries. My daddy was a shrimper. He worked us hard."

"What were your mom and dad like?"

"Simple people. Hard-working. I never heard them argue. My mama is a good Catholic. Maybe a bit of a mystic." He poured two ample glasses of Pinot Grigio and looked at me.

"I don't want to spook you, but my mama swears she has an avenging angel."

"You mean a guardian angel."

"No, avenging angel. Mama believes she can call on an angel to punish evil people," he laughed. "Now, Karen, don't get creeped out. I've never seen an avenging angel, but I have seen evil in men. Seen lots of that in the military. My mama has an unusual devotion to the Virgin Mary. She's very faithful. I never saw her dance with snakes or heal the blind, but I never once questioned her faith."

"I suppose it is possible. I was in the Adoration Chapel not too long ago and I thought I was visited by an angel."

He looked at me then took a piece of French bread from a plate.

"There's a lot of things in this world I don't understand. Maybe we're not meant to."

"Are your folks still alive?"

"Dad died in 2001. Heart attack. Mama still lives in Morgan City. Got a sister and brother there. My oldest brother lives in Baton Rouge."

"You get home much?"

"Sure. Most of the holidays. I fly into Lafayette, rent a car. Easy trip."

"What made you come to Austin? Why not LSU or Tulane in New Orleans?"

"UT is a good school with a sound MFA program. And you know, Karen, I'm not that same kid from Morgan City any more. I've changed; the town hasn't. Just best for all parties to realize that."

"What happened to the Shrimp and Petroleum Queen?"

"You remember everything! Alicia, my first wife. She's still there. She remarried. Has a house full of kids. Football players, baseball players, ballerinas, a homecoming queen. Got the biggest house in town." He looked down at his bowl. "I was gone too much to be married to a woman like that. Funny thing is, the more I stayed away from the second wife, the better she liked it."

The sound of spoons clanked against our bowls as we ate and talked.

"Yeah, I started out being crazy about my ex in the beginning. Didn't take me long to change my mind." *Maybe I shouldn't have said that.* Matt put his spoon down.

"Want another bowl?" he asked, pouring another glass of wine for both of us. *I'm not touching that second glass.*

"No thanks. Sure was delicious."

"Let's put the dishes in the sink and sit in the living room."

"I love your stories about Morgan City. Sounds like *The Adventures of Huck Finn.*" I tucked my sundress underneath my knees and sat on the far end of the white leather sectional, away from him and his maleness.

"Some of it was magical. We did a lot of fishing. I loved the marshes and swamps out near Stephensville. Had a jon boat and a trolling motor. Saved up and bought it with my brother, Louis. The stillness of the water, moving through all the cypress trees. Nothing like it in the world." He sat next to me. "I kissed a lot of pretty Cajun girls, then. Been lucky that way, kissing pretty girls." He leaned over to kiss me. I couldn't help it; I started laughing.

"Are you laughing at me, Karen?"

"No. Maybe. I don't know. That line."

"What line?"

"Kissing girls."

"You know, that's the thing with you. I never know if you're going to cry, slap me or laugh. You're a mess, Karen. And I really don't know why."

"A mess? I'm a mess?"

Matt got up from the couch and walked into the kitchen. He returned with his glass of wine.

"You really don't have any problems, but you react like the sky is falling. I know you're worried about your daughter. We can fix that. The rest is just life, Karen. Try to enjoy it. Not many people get the chance."

Silence. I could feel myself turning red and it embarrassed me even more.

"Well, Matt, I am a mess. I'm supposed to be emotional. I'm an English teacher and a woman. If you wanted a more even-keeled date tonight, I'm sure you could have found a hot-blooded accountant down the road."

"You're a crazy woman, but you make me laugh." He reached over to hug me. This time we kissed.

"Was that so bad?"

"No."

"Let me love you, Karen. That's all. I'm a good guy." He kissed me again.

"Matt, I'm working on some things. I'm not a perfect person. You should know that."

"Really? I'm not either. Hell, we're all the walking wounded, Karen. One way or another. You can cry or you can laugh at the absurdity of life. It's a choice."

"You're making way too much sense to me right now." I kissed him, and he reached for my hand, walking toward the open door of his bedroom.

"I feel like I should ask someone's permission before I go in there."

We both laughed.

The evening grew in its quiet outside the open doors of the

bedroom's balcony. His hands were folded behind his head, resting on the pillow. I had laid mine on his chest, watching the street lights appear out of the window, listening to the steady beat of his heart, and watching the rise and fall of his chest with each breath he took.

"Tell me some more about Morgan City."

"Did I mention it was where the first Tarzan movies were made? Even when I was a kid the vegetation was that lush. I thought every place in the world was like that. Huge trees, lots of places to fish, riding my bike wherever I wanted to go. I guess for a kid, even a poor kid, there were a lot of things to do in that little town. I can remember waking up almost every morning of my childhood excited about the day and what it would bring. Even when my brother and I worked for my daddy, shrimping. Hard work. Hot as hell, and demanding for a kid's body to pull those nets, shovel ice, and clean the boat when we got back. When we weren't shrimping, we were doing maintenance on the boat. Scraping that wooden hull, repainting. Mending nets. But I loved it. I loved it 'cause there was nobody else there but Daddy, me and Louis, out there on the water. There's a certain freedom to being on the water, Karen. It may be the vastness. Sometimes, I really miss it."

He kissed the top of my head, and I closed my eyes to the night.

Carly's Kolache Café offered an open-air view of the river and a smorgasbord of kolaches: apricot, poppy seed, prune, apple, rhubarb, sausage, sausage and jalapeno, sausage and cheese, and for the difficult, gluten free kolaches with organic strawberry jam. My grandmother was rolling in her grave on that last one.

"My grandma used to make kolaches."

"I had to wait 'till I moved to Texas to get my first one."

Grannie was the kolache queen, popping out the sweet, moist bread with cheese or fruit on a daily basis. She never capitalized on her gift, just delivered them to friends and family her entire life, courtesy of the Magic Chef stove in her little frame house in Rosenberg. Her bundles of joy were always delivered on a china plate wrapped in wax paper.

"I loved my grannie a lot. I still miss her."

"You okay this morning?" He reached across the table and took my hand.

"Yeah, you know I live in my head a lot, words kinda pop out randomly."

He laughed. "Yes, just another thing I like about you."

"Oh, I almost forgot. I entered a creative essay in that literary contest."

"Really? The one in New Orleans?"

"Yeah. I probably won't even place, but I thought, why not?"

"That's great. We got to book those flights soon. Conference is in July. It's at the Monteleone Hotel on Royal. That alone makes it worth the effort."

Our waitress appeared with a red bandana around her head, purple high tops on her feet, and a tee shirt reading, CARLY'S KOLACHES—THE OFFICIAL PASTRY OF TEXAS.

We gave our order and I was immediately disappointed. I wanted two sausage and jalapenos kolaches, but I ordered the poppy seed and apple; it seemed a more feminine choice. Heidi or Gretchen, that had to be our waitress' name, hopped back to the table with black coffee in two thick, white ceramic mugs. She paid more attention to Matt than me. She didn't even look at me when I placed my order. Matt was offered fresh cream for his coffee; I got a wad of napkins by my cup. I guess she was expecting a slob like me to spill my coffee.

"What's the title of your essay?"

"Drinking Alone."

"That's a sucker punch."

"Well, yeah, I like my wine, Matt. Trying not to like it so much these days."

"I'm sure a lot of people can identify with that, Karen. You might just win that essay contest."

"Tell me about the Monteleone." I quickly changed the

subject. *None of your business, Matt Broussard, how much wine I drink.*

"It's an old hotel in the Quarter with a literary history. Capote, Faulkner, Hemingway. The greats slept and wrote there."

"I love it already."

"The hotel bar is quite famous, The Carousel. Yes, true to grandiose Southern style, it's a mini carousel, moving around ever so slightly the booze and the patrons."

"I'll book my flight from Houston and meet you at the hotel. I'm sure it's not cheap, but it's been a while since I've done something just for the fun of it."

"Should be a lot of fun," Matt sipped his coffee, staring at the walking trail following the river. "Let's finish breakfast and walk."

"Sure." *I'd rather order more kolaches and read the morning paper. This guy is a beef stick. All action, all the time.*

Chapter Twenty-eight
Adios

I sat in my car looking at Tiffany's apartment complex at least an hour before I knocked on the door. The palm tree in front of the complex office was dead—a stump of tropical fiber with brown palm fronds on the ground. Corrugated plastic signs screaming ONE MONTH FREE RENT swayed in the wind on their skinny, metal legs. The final hurrah of last night lay on the ground by the dumpster—delivery pizza boxes and beer cans. Why did I think anything would change in a few months? Still, I had hoped beyond hope that she wouldn't be living like this.

I thought of Leona; Leona the little girl without a mother or father, crouched in the foothills of Buda in the dark. Leona, floating on the Danube, hungry and dirty. Her hope as faint and distant as stars in a winter night. Praying for the GI, a magician who could pull food, water, and a roof out of his helmet. What kept her from giving up during all the days, weeks, and months of misery? Was it faith, secure in her heart and hallowed stomach, a savior would rescue her? Was that savior God or an American GI? *My sweet friend, you have taught me so much about living and yes, how to be a woman.*

I got out of the car, put the keys in my pocket, leaving my purse on the floorboard. I wouldn't be in there long.

I knocked on door #216, then flicked the peeling red paint off with my fingernails, waiting for someone to answer.

"Hey." She opened the door and hugged me. I wouldn't let her pull away from me. I held on to her, so I could hear her breathing, so I could listen to her heart.

"Where's Jared?"

"Asleep. Come on in, but be quiet."

"It's two in the afternoon."

"Well, he's tired, I guess."

When I followed her into the kitchen with its single 120-watt bulb over the table, I picked up her arm.

"What happened?"

She didn't answer me. She avoided my eyes.

"What happened?" I said louder. I wanted him to wake up and give me the answer to my question.

"Don't start anything, Karen. I'm tired."

"I can see that. I can see the bruises. I can see the filth you're living in. Oh, and let's see what's in the refrigerator?" I yanked open the refrigerator door, opening it wide, revealing white electric coolness, and nothing else. "Of course, it's empty."

"Get up, Jared. We're leaving. Get out of bed, now," I screamed into the bedroom.

He emerged from the dark room, scratching his head and adjusting his boxers.

"You see this? You see this?" I held up Tiffany's arm and flung the refrigerator door open again. "Nothing. Nothing here but meanness. I'll not have it. She's my daughter, Jared. My daughter, and she's pregnant with your child."

"What's going on in here?" He sat down at the kitchen table, holding his head up in his two hands.

"I better not find another bruise on her, Jared. You hear me." I stood between him and the opened refrigerator. "Tiffany, pack your clothes, books, makeup. You got ten minutes. We're leaving. You, Jared, you look around. The juicer, electric can opener, and used furniture are yours to keep as a memento. I'm taking my mother's quilt." I yanked the quilt off the couch. "Yes, Jared, you take a look around. Look at everything, because Tiffany, the baby, you're going to miss them every single day for the rest of your life."

He jumped up from the table, knocked the chair over, and rushed at me.

"Tiffany isn't going anywhere."

"Oh, no you don't. My ex is a lawyer, and he loves money more than anything else in the world. We'll see you in a Houston courtroom. And that little dive you call a business, Ink & Juice? I'll calling the health department on you."

Tiffany appeared with her purse, a backpack, and an un-zipped duffle bag with clothes spilling out of it. Lifeless or resigned to whatever anyone told her, I couldn't figure it out, but she walked out the door when I opened it for her. Apartment 216 became just a bad memory for her.

Chapter Twenty-nine
An Unfortunate Day for Jared Crain

In the devious world of petty criminals and government agencies, one call does it all. The demise of Jared Crain and the Ink & Juice began when I called The Texas Department of Health Services Rogue Restaurant Hot-Line. Lucky for me, and very unlucky for Jared, Ms. Lupe Rojas, health department employee extraordinaire, was given the case to investigate. The final report submitted by Ms. Rojas was rich with imagery and irony. I re-read the report over and over, imaging each little scene as if it were a movie. Lupe Rojas was my hero.

It wasn't just that Lupe had a work ethic; Lupe was a rabid disciple with twenty-five years with the Texas Department of Health Services. For seventeen of those years, she had received "Employee of the Year." Her training in food pathogens made her a legend at the health department and a woman feared among Austin eating establishments. Lupe took no prisoners in her single-woman campaign to rid Austin of greasy spoons with roach-infested kitchens and juice bars with unwashed blenders serving colored corn syrup instead of fruit juice.

At 9:05 a.m. Lupe stood in front of the Ink & Juice . Her department-issued backpack held the tools necessary to complete her mission: an electronic tablet, several pairs of rubber gloves, and a paperback edition of the *Texas Food Establishment Rules*, with bright orange and green colored tabs marking Chapter Eleven, "Food Preparation for Fruits and Vegetables," and Chapter

Twelve, "Sulfating Agents Used on Raw Fruit and Vegetable Consumption."

Lupe patted her backpack and looked at yesterday's text message from the department's secretary: "Anonymous caller; customer made sick by carrot juice at Ink & Juice, 349 Guadalupe."

Lupe opened the door and spotted a white male in his twenties behind the juice bar. *Who in the hell would write a permit for this place? A tattoo parlor and a juice bar under one roof? These places are choking Austin, no thanks to John Lamey's tenure. I'll be cleaning up his bad decisions for the next ten years. Should have fired that lazy gringo years ago. I guess this kid at the bar is the owner. Look at him, hollowed eyed and vampire skin from never seeing the light of day. Looks like he sleeps in his clothes.*

"Are you Jared Crain?"

"Yes."

"Lupe Rojas with the health department. We've been getting complains about this place making people sick. I'm here to do an inspection." Lupe sat her backpack on a bar stool and snapped her rubber gloves in place.

"Hey, wait a minute. Aren't you supposed to call first? I'm down an employee; I haven't had a chance to clean up yet."

"We don't make appointments, Mr. Crain. Where's the kitchen or is this it?"

Lupe finished her inspection of the Ink & Juice in exactly two hours. She sat in her state-issued minivan with the AC turned up high. With her black hair whipping around her face in the Freon-cooled air, she typed away on her tablet.

TFER code violations 227.66g, 227.66h, 228.66a, 22867.b, and 228.68.c. Recommend immediate closing and fines for all violations, with an estimated $32,000. Note: while inspecting the food storage area in an enclosed room, I counted 132 laptop computers. I will notify the proper authorities concerning the laptops.

When her report was finished, Lupe placed her tablet back in her backpack with a satisfying zip. She put the minivan in drive and headed for the police station on Eighth Street where her brother Detective Emmanuel Rojas worked in the burglary division.

Within two weeks, the Ink & Juice was closed and Jared Crain was arrested for harboring stolen property, 132 laptops. Once the investigation was over, Detective Rojas uncovered a ring of criminal gamers involving a Dell employee and the owner of the Ink & Juice. Adam Stanson, formerly of Dallas, pilfered hardware processors from his day job at Dell, hidden in his lunch box, a Seventies-vintage metal box featuring a dancing Snoopy. In exchange for cash, Adam delivered the goods to Jared, who loaded stolen laptops he purchased from druggies off the street, a pennies-on-the-dollar, untraceable exchange. Within a few days, thanks to Jared's technology skills, gamers stationed in hotels and hovels around Austin were set with the best technology Dell could offer.

The only luck left for Adam and Jared as former business partners is they'd do time at the Huntsville Unit of the Texas State Penitentiary, occasionally enjoying each other's company for a pick-up game of basketball inside the razor-wired fence. Jared would soon forget about Tiffany and their baby, serving their own time together in the Heights, less than seventy miles away.

The only time Tiffany asked about him was on the second night she was back in Houston.

"Why doesn't he love me?" she cried into the Dutch-Doll pattern quilt my grandmother made for me as a high school graduation gift. Max slept, curled at her feet, while Poncho purred on the pillow next to her.

"Honey, a guy like that is too young to know what love is. Jared had a full-time job just taking care of himself. I can imagine your hurt right now, but I do promise, it will get better in time. In time, you'll see Jared for who he is, not who you wanted him to be. Just rest, honey. Just rest."

I sat on the edge of the bed watching her until she fell asleep.

She looked so young, so child-like, despite the fading bruises on her arm and the rising and falling of an extended stomach, as she breathed deeply into a sound sleep.

I turned out the lamp on her night stand and walked out of the room, leaving the door slightly open in case she called for me. In case she needed me.

In the kitchen, I brewed a cup of Chai tea. As I stirred milk into the liquid warmth, the smell of cloves and cinnamon filled the kitchen. I felt a comfort in this simple task I rarely found in a glass of wine. I was a slow learner, but I was learning. This was the house of slow learners. Like Sisyphus, Tiffany and I kept rolling that boulder up the hill, thinly disguised as alcoholism and insecurity, only to have to do it again the next day, with the same amount of effort. We kept trying to be the winners at the top of the hill. Some days we couldn't make it out of the foothills.

I'd need Leona to help me in the weeks to come. There were doctor appointments to make, the transfer of Tiffany's credits from UT, and the building of a nursery for the baby.

Her front porch light was still on across the street. It was only 9:15, not too late to call.

She picked up after the second ring, like she always does.

"Leona, it's not too late, is it?" I hated formalities, but with her, it was everything.

"No. How is she?"

"Resting. Thanks for taking care of Max and Poncho while I was gone. Look. I'm going to need your help, still. I hate to ask, but I just can't take another day off."

"Karen. I will make sure she is okay. I'll make a nice beef and vegetable soup for her tomorrow. I have a soup bone in the freezer I've saved just for this."

"I don't like to order you around, Leona. I just, I just can't be here all day."

"I know that. I knew that before you even brought her home. I'll take good care of her. Go to work. Don't worry."

"What can I do for you?

"Everything in life isn't an even exchange, Karen. I will take care of her. Enough now. I have a lot to do before I can go to bed tonight." She hung up before I could say anything else.

From that initial statement, "I will take care of her," a relationship of a grandmother and her beloved granddaughter was forged in shopping for maternity clothes, preparing meals, and registering Tiffany for classes at Houston Community College, Central Campus.

When I cautioned them about the amount of money spent or the simple fact they were never home, Leona put me in my place.

"Karen, let her take the classes, spend some money. It doesn't matter if it's toward a degree or not. Why must there always be a greater plan? There's no reason she should hide in this house until the baby comes. Activity is good for her and the child."

I felt excluded at times, but I couldn't be jealous. I could only marvel at the love they had for each other. The sacred bond they shared was the acknowledgment they had both been abandoned as children. I could never understand what that felt like. Because they understood each other's pain, they became very close. They began to heal.

Chapter Thirty
Someone I Used to Love

"We're having a baby, too," proclaimed Greg. I looked at him and then I looked at Barbara. She wasn't pregnant. She had to be in her late forties, and there was no visible bump, let alone swollen ankles and purple varicose veins climbing up her calves.

"We have a surrogate mother," Barbara said, staring back at me.

"Why, of course you do," I said.

"Honey," she purred in Greg's ears, "I have some emails to return. I'll let you two talk." She oozed out of the room, D cup and twenty-four-inch waist.

"Don't make me beg. I need the money for Tiffany."

"I'm not, Karen." Greg crossed his legs in the leather wing-back chair in the study of his serene, gated-community home. He finally got what he wanted, garden gnomes and all. He smiled. I remembered that smile. The first time I saw that smile I was twenty-one years old with my entire life ahead of me. It had the same effect on me now as it did then. My breath quickened and I believed in all the possibilities that smile could offer.

"Why didn't you want a baby with me, Greg? Excuse me for asking after all these years, but I was married to you first. There was a time we couldn't keep our hands off each other. Why didn't you want a baby with me?"

"You didn't want a baby, Karen. You had Tiffany plus all the kids at school. There wasn't room for me, let alone a baby."

I felt the tears immediately.

"It doesn't matter anyway. Not now. Forget I even asked."

"You were too much, Karen. Too much. I just wanted to enjoy my life, the things money could give us, but not you; every day was a mission for you. Charge the hill. Feed the hungry. Clothe the naked. Educate the masses. You wore me out."

I looked at him and smiled through the tears. "Well, that's also what attracted you to me in the first place. I guess we've changed."

"I'm writing a check for $25,000. That should get you started on the addition to the house. Buy some baby things. It's a loan, not a gift. Pay me back."

"I could take it out of my 401K, but it's going to hurt in penalties. But I need the money. Now. Thanks for the loan. Any more news of Jared, the gamer-chef turned criminal?"

"I'm still considering some things, but Mr. Crain will be serving time in Huntsville for the stolen laptops, as well as paying hefty fines for health department violations. For equal measure, I filed a restraining order to keep him away from Tiffany. Amazing how it all hit at the same time."

"Yes, amazing."

Greg handed me a folded check and stood up.

"Don't let this be your new mission. Help her, of course. But don't you think it's time you found someone. You deserve some happiness." He reached out and hugged me. I could have stayed there and willed him back to me. But it was too late. I thought of Matt.

"I'm seeing someone. He's actually a nice guy."

"Good. Well, take care of yourself, Karen. My love to Tiff."

Out of Greg and Barbara's massive glass front door, I hopped off the porch with his check in my purse. *I'm sad. He was someone I used to love.*

"I want everyone at my house for Sunday dinner." Leona stood at my front door in a yellow-and-black pantsuit giving her the appearance of a bumblebee on steroids, but at least her eyebrows were perfectly arched.

"Everyone? As in Kelly and Carl? Last time you mentioned Kelly, you called her a tasteless tramp. I don't know if Tiffany will be up to being around everyone."

"I'm bonding our family unit, Karen. Call everyone. Dinner will be served at 6:00 p.m."

Poncho and Max sniffed her ankles. "Nice puppy." She scratched Max behind his left ear, but ignored Poncho. The cat returned the slight with an uplifted tail that curved around Leona's black pant leg, leaving wiry grey cat hair. "Filthy animal." With that, she was gone.

I closed the front door, sat on the couch, and watched her walk across the street. Fearless. The woman was fearless. Her motto for living was "modify and adjust." *Modify and adjust. You're right, Leona. In less than a year, Tiffany was pregnant, college was on hold, I forgave my ex, and I fell in love at fifty. At least I was living—modifying and adjusting every step of the way.*

My weekend in New Orleans was fast approaching. I had placed in the top ten in the essay competition, while Matt was short listed, with a promise of cash and a publishing contract. The final decision would be made at the award ceremony next month. He deserved it. All of it.

Meanwhile, we made plans for the baby's arrival. Carl was hired to build a small addition to Tiffany's bedroom, knocking out a wall for a larger closet with room for a changing table and bassinet.

Tiffany decided to return to school for twelve hours a semester once the baby arrived. Leona would babysit during the day, and I was good for any evening classes Tiffany took.

It all looked so good in theory, beautiful on a calendar of events. But there was the specter in my glass of wine telling me that just as quickly, it would all change, and I deserved nothing more than to sleep alone for the rest of my life, and Tiffany and her baby would return to Austin.

*   *   *

"Pass the mashed potatoes, Leona." Leona gave Carl a big smile and passed the Bavarian china bowl heaping with Yukon Gold potatoes whipped to a fluffy peak with a hand mixer. A modest puddle of butter rested in the center. Leona was in her element, head of the table, matriarch of a family she'd spent her life praying for. The divorced, the abused, the alcoholic, the wanton—humanity's finest hour, sat at her table. Our bloodline was the tribe of man; our commonality, the bond of friendship.

"Tiffany, dear, what do you think about a baby shower? You can invite some of your friends; I will be the hostess. You choose your colors and theme. I will decorate accordingly."

"Thank you, Ms. Leona. I need a lot of stuff." It was the most normal response I heard from Tiffany since she had been home. Her actual voice startled me for a moment.

"We can all help with the baby shower, Leona," Kelly said, tugging at the ripped hem of her red tee shirt that read, AMERICA: LOVE IT OR LEAVE IT. She refused the passing of the potato bowl, the second time she had done so, choosing the carrot salad with pineapple tidbits, which she plucked one by one from the bowl with her fingers.

"Well, yes, of course, Kelly." The big smile was gone from Leona's face, replaced with a stiffened spine. She lowered her head for a moment and everyone froze at the table.

"You all right, Leona?" I offered, standing up next to her.

"I'm dizzy and sick to my stomach."

Carl stood next to me. "Let me help you to the couch, Leona. You cooked a huge meal for us and probably haven't rested all day."

"No, no, I'm okay." The four of us stared at her. She lifted her head and stared straight at Kelly. "We will not serve alcohol at the baby shower." With that delivery, she stood up and began removing serving pieces from the table. Dinner was over.

Chapter Thirty-one
All the World's a Stage

I stared at the stuffed jaguar on Kenny's bookshelf waiting for him to show for our scheduled meeting.

Heights Central High School's fierce mascot, the jaguar had been reduced to a hand-sized stuffed animal covered in dust. It was flanked on both sides by two trophies claiming "Kenny Ramsey, Coach of the Year, Harris County, Texas, 2008-2009," and "Coach of the Year, Harris County, Texas, 2010-2011." Accolades of his academic and managerial prowess were nonexistent in the office, draped by Texas A&M banners and a HCHS jaguar flag.

The door behind me opened and closed with a bang.

"What are we talking about today, Karen?" He sat down and leaned as far back as he could in his chair. Clearly, he had just returned from the men's room, as his pants were unzipped.

"The field trip for my English III students. Why didn't you sign off on it? I put it in four months ago."

"I was hoping you'd forget about it." He leaned into his desk and I heard the distinctive zzzz; his open fly was gone.

"Why would I do that? They worked hard this year. We're just going to a theatre near Greenway Plaza, a couple of miles down the road. We'll be back in a few hours."

"What's the educational purpose here? Go down the road, see a half-baked play, back home. I don't find it worth the risk of taking that many kids off campus."

"Because most of them have never been in a theatre, Kenny. That's why. Let us go. By the way, I need the football boosters' bus to get us there."

"Now, this is what you don't get, Karen, so I'll spell it out for you. Those kids don't put in the time the football team does or any sports team at this school. Your kids might show up for class. They might read the assignment. They might do the homework. And, they might graduate. The players, they are giving their all, every day, in the heat, cold, and rain. One hundred and ten percent, every day."

"All right. I get it, Kenny. Your kids walk a mile in a blizzard each day to throw a football; mine are cooking meth behind the football stadium. But do those athletes know the bus was purchased by reselling food from the cafeteria? Let me state it in a clearer manner. Food purchased by the feds was stolen from the cafeteria by coaches here at good 'ole Heights Central. You forget I've been around a long time. Get me the bus and sign the permission slip. I'm taking my students to see a play."

The bus stood in the mid-morning April sunshine with Joel Perez the first one on and the first to claim the back seat.

"Joel, don't get on yet. I've got to check everyone's name off."

"You just saw me. Check my name off."

"Joel, get off."

They lined the length of the bus, the curious, bored, stoned, and excited. All forty-seven of them, who claimed they'd never seen a "real play," but could recall with great detail every bit part they played in a school production since kindergarten.

The Madness of Poe, the combined one-act plays dramatizing "Annabel Lee," "The Raven," and "The Cask of Amontillado" was performed by a traveling troupe of young actors and actresses, recently graduated from obscure drama departments in the Midwest.

Every year of my teaching career, the students' immediate connection to poetry was Edgar Allen Poe. It could have been his tortured life of drug addiction, gambling, and unrequited love. It could have been the haunted imagery of his work. Year after year my students enjoyed Poe, but this was the first year we'd see the work performed. It was the first time all year Raul arrived on time. He gave me a nod at the back of the line.

"The rules are simple for this field trip. Don't smoke, drink or engage in any illegal activity on the field trip. Break it, and I'll have HPD pick you up." As I called a name, a student hopped onto the bus.

When the bus parked in front of Back Alley Theatre, a collective "cool" rose from the seats of the bus. The students were impressed by the black building with its double red door entry. A large, black-and-white banner hung from the flat roof to the top of the double doors. A sketch of a weary Poe with one head in his hand and the words, THE MADNESS OF POE illustrated the banner. Poe and teenage angst were bedfellows.

I called and checked the same forty-seven names I had started with. All forty-seven made it from the HCHS parking lot to the front of the red doors. *Check!*

"Go straight to the theatre and find a seat. No lone wolf sitting apart from the group. Ten minutes 'til curtain call."

I watch them move through the building. Some stared at play production posters; others stared at the closed concession stand. Three girls veered toward the women's restroom. I stood in the lobby waiting for them to find their way to the theatre.

In the cool dark of the theater, they sat together, whispering. An occasional outburst of laughter, followed by hushing, broke the hum of the group. The curtains rose and a single spot light shone on a haggard man bent over a small wooden desk with a pencil in his hand. He wrote furiously, then grabbed the paper, crumbled it, and threw it on the floor. In the background, the sound of a human heart became louder. The spotlight went blood red, then out into complete darkness.

The first act began with two men drinking wine in carnival masks. "Let us have another glass, my dear Fortunato," the young actor sang out, and we, the audience, were completely lost in the magic of live theatre.

The last act was based on the poem, "Annabel Lee." The child-like maiden, ethereal Annabel Lee wandered the stage with its cardboard waves and suspended angels from the lighting frame, as off-stage fans created an intense wind entwined with fog produced by dry ice. The roar of the oscillating blades almost drowned out the dialogue, but Raul managed to halt the production all by himself.

He gave a honking blow into the washcloth he always carried in his back pocket. Every head in the theatre turned in his direction. After the "Shut up, man, you're ruining it" died down, all attention returned to the stage and Annabel Lee's grieving lover, who did a quick look in the audience, searching for the uncultured slob who made him lose his pace.

I was in desperate need of a glass of wine from the anxiety of additional honks from Raul. I did a quick surveillance of all the students. All accounted for. This performance was the last one-act play in the trilogy. Just a few more minutes to go, then I'd corral them back on the bus.

A quick head count and everyone was accounted for on the bus. It was a successful venture by all accounts. My very own peanut gallery was introduced to live theatre and they loved it. No cabbages or rotten potatoes were thrown at the stage. Raul's nose blowing was a small interruption when considering what a group of teenagers were capable of.

All of it was worth it to me—fighting Kenny for permission and blackmailing him for the bus, if at least one day, somewhere in their adult lives, my students will remember the field trip, and the magic of a live performance. They got to be somebody for a day.

I closed my eyes as the bus pulled out of the theatre parking lot. A few deep breaths and a few miles down the road, I was back at Heights Central High School. Today was Friday. School was almost out, and Matt Broussard was my boyfriend. Sticky note to self: a small glass of champagne was worthy of my good fortune.

Chapter Thirty-two
Hold the Mayo

The last day of school was a stormy one. It was the beginning of the subtropic summer in Houston with hot, humid air meeting cold air masses, sending racks of thunder through dark skies. I loved thunderstorms. It cooled everything off and forced people to slow down and observe.

My love of thunderstorms came from my childhood, when my grandmother would gather me up and we'd sit together on her front porch in Rosenberg, watching the sky rage over the earth. I was never afraid. She had taught me the importance of rain. It was a blessing, not a nuisance. Rain gave life to the crops and flowers all around us, my grandmother lovingly reassured me from her porch swing.

Students ran through the open courtyards at school, hydroplaning in their flip-flops. Loud laughter erupted from the boys, followed by shrieks from the girls. It was timeless and joyful.

It stopped as suddenly as it started. The sky above was blue, with the temperature ten degrees cooler. Everything, the grass, the hedges, the trees, even the people, seemed a bit brighter.

The last day of school was always bittersweet for me. I was exhausted beyond words, but I would miss my students, wondering if the summer would dramatically change their lives without the relative safety and structured routine of school every day. Who would get pregnant? Who would be arrested? Who would never come back at all?

"Come on. End of year faculty meeting in the cafeteria. Football boosters are providing sandwiches and drinks," Kelly said, wearing a purple tee shirt with a picture of Alice Cooper and the words SCHOOL'S OUT FOR SUMMER below his mug shot. She paired the tee shirt with a pleated black skirt above the knees with black-and-white saddle oxfords and white knee socks. She must have discovered a new resale shop this past weekend.

"Right. Need to grab a few things. I'll meet you there. Save me a seat."

The cafeteria was packed with teachers, coaches, administrators, and support staff. Just like the students, we divided ourselves into subgroups, sitting with those of our own tribe.

I waited in line with the others at a cafeteria table loaded with sub sandwiches, bags of chips, and cookies. At the end of the table was a large ice chest of canned drinks and bottled water.

I filled my paper plate with all. I was not calorie-counting when my mind and body was ravaged by emotion and exhaustion. I needed the carbs and sugar to get me back to the house.

"When is this meeting scheduled to start?" A voice of rebellion rose from the buffet line. I looked at my watch. *It's a quarter 'til four. Where's Kenny?*

Kelly was busy deconstructing her sub. She hated tomatoes, wilted lettuce, and despised white bread. In the end, she had a piece of processed cheese and ham that could stand on their own thanks to the preservatives they were loaded with. She rolled the two together in a cylinder shape and popped it in her mouth.

"He's got ten more minutes and I'm out of here. Tiffany's at the house. Matt's got her car and is driving it to Houston tonight. Got things to do."

"Yeah, the engineer and I have plans to replace the shocks on my car."

I laughed. "You say that with zero resignation, as if you're thrilled with the weird relationship you have with this guy."

"I am thrilled. Why shouldn't I be?"

"Hey, there's Kenny." Carl was standing at the row of opened windows near the buffet table.

"Throw him a sandwich, Carl," I offered. The cafeteria roared.

"He heard that, Karen," Carl said, closing the window in front of him. "Actually, it stopped him in his tracks. Sucks being you."

During the entire one-hour meeting, which could have been done in twenty minutes, Kenny stared at me. Finally, he launched into the grand finale speech, which began and ended the same way each year.

"People, come back rested and ready to work. Come back with new lesson plans. Stop teaching the same crap you've been teaching for the last twenty years. Don't forget to sign the card, thanking the HCHS Football Boosters."

I was almost out of the cafeteria when I felt a hand on my shoulder. It was him.

"Have a good summer, Karen," Kenny offered without a smile. I knew immediately I was teaching nothing but English I next year. My class roster would come from a list the Guidance Department kept of troubled students. Composed of habitual troublemakers fresh from the juvenile delinquent roosters of the middle school, these students would torture me every day, and Kenny would love it.

I got out to the parking lot without saying another word to him. The farther I walked away, the lighter I felt. I made it to my car, where a thin paperback book was wedged between the windshield and the hood. *The Wit and Wisdom of Samuel Johnson.* I opened the inside cover and read what was written in scrawling black ink, "Don't forget to do some living, Ms. Anders. Peace, Joel Perez."

I stood there a long time watching the other teachers back up and drive away, then passing by me with a honk of the horn or a hand waving out an open window. *Joel Perez. I won't forget to do some living. God, I love that kid!*

Chapter Thirty-three
Hot Dogs and Hand Grenades

The hundred-percent humidity, mixed in the bizarre cocktail of ninety-degree heat, fried seafood and street music matted my hair against my neck, caused my feet to swell outside of the confines of my espadrilles, and stirred a sensuality that lay dormant since perimenopause. Thirty minutes on the ground from Houston to New Orleans' French Quarter and the culture of *Laissez les bon temps rouler* surged through my veins.

The cab driver pulled in front of the Hotel Monteleone. The brochure I picked up in the airport claimed the grand dame of hotels had resided on Royal Street since 1886, still locally owned. When the cab pulled to the curb, I leaped out onto the street, staring at the hotel's front entrance of natural stone, European in-laid carvings, and multinational flags snapping in the breeze. The main lobby was a hushed interior of Southern opulence unashamedly displayed in chandeliers, towering flower arrangements, and antiquities from around the world. My soul uttered "Ahhhh" when the glass doors closed on the world behind me.

Matt had arrived the day before as a short-listed winner for the literary contest. Officially, I was a finalist. No prize, but an invitation to come if I wanted to pay my own way. Matt was my prize. With permission from Leona, with her newly arched eyebrows raised in caution against sin city New Orleans, I left Tiffany and the pets in good hands.

Matt had texted me the hotel room number the night

before. I looked it up again, pushing the elevator button to the fourth floor. Room 412 stood in front of me. *Should I knock or just open the door?* I knocked.

He opened the door widely and took my carry-on bag from me. I stood in the center of the room.

"Here. I bought you something." He handed me a large white box tied with a red ribbon bow.

"A feathered boa?" I laughed, opening it.

He placed the DO NOT DISTURB sign on the exterior door handle and closed the door.

The evening lights of the Quarter shone through the sheer curtains of the hotel room.

"Hungry?"

He was sitting at a tiny desk with gold inlay in the carvings of its legs. He was beautiful in the evening cast of shadows, black thick hair, black eyes framed by black-and-gray brows, a sensuous mouth. Beautiful, smart, and kind. Matt was a rarity amongst the middle-aged frat daddies and mommas' boys of my former dating circle.

"Yes, very hungry. The only thing I've eaten are the pretzels the flight attendant threw at me on the plane."

"Good. It's our only night to do what we want here. The literary events start tomorrow with a formal dinner at the hotel. Let's have a drink downstairs and talk about tonight's meal."

The Carousel Bar, with its view of Royal Street, offered patrons a ride on a twenty-five seat, circus-themed Merry-Go-Round, perpetually spinning, with a rose-colored glass view of the hotel's entry and street life in the Quarter.

"The house specialty is Sazerac."

"So, it would be a *faux pas* to order a glass of house red?"

"Just enjoy. I got this, Karen."

The bartender placed two small glasses in front of us. No ice. The glass was filled halfway with an orange-amber liquid that changed its color to gold at the bottom of the glass. An orange peel carved into a curl rested on the rim of the glass.

"What's in this?"

"It's probably one of the oldest cocktails in this country, in New Orleans, for sure. It's named for the Cognac brandy used as its main ingredient, then a little rye, absinthe, bitters, and sugar."

"Isn't absinthe the drink that made a lot of French artists crazy?"

"It was popular with the bohemian crowd in nineteenth-century France. Manet, Degas, Lautrec, all lapped it up. Was banned in France at one time for its harmful effect. What you're drinking is a different variety. No one's trying to poison you."

"So, it's something to sip." I smiled and repositioned myself on the bar stool, taking a deep breath as a meditative measure to slow the entire evening to something I could manage. Single women walked in and out of the bar dressed in sheer fabrics of muted colors. Their appearance was as exaggerated as the hotel's. Masses of long, thick black hair to the small of their backs or piled carelessly on top of their heads, with loose strands caressing their necks like the serpentine Hydra. Black, heavy eyeliner encircled their eyes, with lips shaded in classic red. On their feet were impossibly high heels, strappy and expensive. The women of New Orleans were unapologetic in their femininity.

When the second round of the amber drink with the orange peel arrived in front of me, I was making a little chant in my head, "The women come and go . . ."

Don't be a Prufrock, Karen. Don't go into the interior. Do some living, wrote Joel Perez. Apply it to the evening. I took a sip of the golden concoction and turned toward Matt. "Let's finish our drink and take a walk. I'm sure since the sun's gone down, it's gotten a lot cooler."

"Okay. I was thinking of taking you to the Napoleon House for dinner. It's a decent walk from here. We'll call a cab if we need too." He picked up his glass and with a long, languid drink, finished it.

I followed suit and felt my entire being come aglow with the amber liquid. I wondered if there was an aura above my head that everyone could see and admire.

*   *   *

It was a quarter after nine, and we still hadn't made our way to the Napoleon House and the celebrated cocktail known as the Pimm's Cup. Matt swore it was better than the Sazerac.

Technically, it was less than a mile away, but we were waylaid by the Hurricanes at Pat O'Brien's. Its courtyard was a lush green with brick walls smothered in blooming Confederate Jasmine.

The waitress seated us at a black wrought table with two matching chairs. We had entered a fairyland for adults with lovely cocktails and fragrant flowers—the madness of the French Quarter was somewhere beyond the brick walls.

In the dim, artificial light, I slurped my Hurricane, a lethal concoction of passionfruit and rum, with a straw. The immediate effect gave us a sugar rush that pushed us onward to Bourbon Street, where more adventure and booze was just around the corner.

The juxtaposition of a man carrying a huge wooden cross with wheels next to strip clubs and store fronts with service windows offering forty-eight-ounce plastic cups of beer and cocktails caused the first wave of nausea to wash over me.

"You all right?" Matt pulled me directly in front of him as the marauders pushed against us, forcing us to stumble along with them.

"The people-watching is incredible. It's like a sea of humanity, either drunk or stone-cold sober."

"Don't take it seriously, Karen. Nothing to analyze here, except people trying to have a good time or save your soul. You think you need to eat something? We might find a Lucky Dog cart near Jackson Square."

I followed him through Pirate's Alley, a snake-like street behind St. Louis Cathedral.

"Look, there it is," Matt yanked my arm forward, pointing to a bright yellow cart shaped like a hot dog. The portable eatery was complete with a cheerful red-and-yellow umbrella as a roof against rain or bright sunshine.

"Two dogs with mustard," Matt said to the troll operating the cart. I noticed the troll didn't put on any gloves, exchanging the cash for hot dogs with the same hand.

Matt handed me a hot dog swimming in bright yellow mustard. I immediately put it in my mouth; in two bites, it was gone. The white mushy bun soaked up the alcohol in my stomach like a sponge. The wave of nausea ceased.

Matt smiled at me. "Hey, you got mustard on your chin." He wiped it away with a finger and delivered a kiss. "Let's head back to Bourbon, then the hotel."

"Is this it for dinner?"

"We can always order room service later."

Yes, I was still hungry, but I didn't want him to know I couldn't survive on alcohol and peanuts from a bar. The death march continued with crowded streets and stumbling drunks. Count me in among them.

We stepped up a small concrete curb on Bourbon Street. Above my head, Tropical Isle was aglow in bright green-and-yellow neon next to a neon parrot. Below that in pulsating neon was HOME OF THE HAND GRENADE. My response to my new surroundings was immediate.

"Do I want to drink something called a hand grenade?"

"Why not; you might like it." Matt waved a twenty-dollar bill at the bartender.

I woke up in Room 412 with a towel wrapped around my neck and the ice bucket on the floor next to me. It hurt when I blinked my eyes, adjusting them to the sunlight outside the hotel room. My head was pounding; a pounding caused by an evil troll with a hot dog cart and an endless supply of cocktails with formidable names. Somewhere in the recesses of my molasses-thick mind was a neon parrot and a flashing lime-green hand grenade. I focused on the ice bucket next to the bed. I was going to be sick. Again.

Chapter Thirty-four
Guess Who's Coming to Dinner?

The Crescent City Literary Competition Award Dinner called for all attendees to dress as their favorite literary character or author. The Queen Ann Ballroom, with its 36 x 54 coat of arms entry, revealed a slightly intoxicated, bantering world of Hemingway, Capote, Scout Finch, Boo Radley, Scott and Zelda, and the beautiful, Holly Golightly. Francis Macomber was chatting it up with a bespeckled Truman outside the men's restroom.

Standing at the cash-only bar was Blanche Dubois holding a paper lantern and a tumbler of whiskey. Next to her was Scarlett O'Hara in a gorgeous white gown with an emerald green sash tied around her waist. She must have spent a fortune on the rental fee. Of the two, Blanche was the most convincing, and probably the most heartbreaking with the fragile paper lantern she held by a string, twirling around and around her finger.

At a dark table along the ballroom wall sat bad-boy Alex of *A Clockwork Orange*, wearing the black bowler and signature heavy eye makeup accenting one eye. Next to him was Ignatius Reilly. To their left was the band.

The entertainment for the night was a band of gypsies. No pun intended. With three violinists, a stand-up bass, and a drummer, the musicians were dressed alike in tight black velvet pants, matching blazers, purple shirts with a ruffled front, and multiple neck scarves, trailing to the carpet. A wild, black mass of curly hair topped their heads. Were they brothers? This only led me to wonder about the woman who produced such a clan. Nothing about this evening was normal or predictable.

Matt and I wore Venetian-designed Mardi Gras masks of black silk and feathers fastened with black ribbons, trailing to the center of our backs. We scanned the ballroom, wondering where we should sit, when the pre-dinner entertainment walked across a stage centered in the front of the room.

Madame Z was a buxom blonde from Vicksburg, Mississippi claiming to be a third cousin of William Faulkner, and a multi-generational clairvoyant. Now, there's a family business that can predict its success! She never explained what the Z stood for.

Matt and I took a seat with Alex, Ignatius, Hemingway and a husband-and-wife team wearing face masks of ancient Greek theatre. The husband chose Melpomene, the muse of Tragedy, while his wife wore the mask of Thalia, the muse of Comedy. They were definitely in the economy seats on imagination and money spent on a costume.

Madame Z positioned herself in a high-backed, overstuffed chair. She was dressed in a purple-and-black paisley print mumu with a lot of bulky costume jewelry around her neck and wrists, and a huge purple ring on her right index finger. On her head was a black terry cloth turban with a sunburst rhinestone pin centered above her forehead.

It must have been her loud twang erupting into random fits of laughter that caused the turban to move on her head. I concentrated on the turban and its path of descent into her abundant lap for the first ten minutes of the act. I lost my patience quickly with Madame Z and her lame performance.

"I shall conjure the ghost of Faulkner by drinking his favorite beverage." Madame Z poured two fingers from a bottle of Jack Daniels.

"You idiot. Faulkner drank Four Roses Bourbon," Alex bellowed from the table, slapping his walking stick against his chair.

"I thought so too," I added, introducing myself to him.

"I'm a poet behind this face makeup. John Shaver, Chicago. I'm a fan of Burgess and Faulkner. Tonight, I insist on you calling me Alex."

Matt shot a look at me and mouthed, "Crazy poet, stay away."

When Alex stood up to get another drink, I saw a jockstrap worn on the outside of his all white clothing. He was a confident man to do the full costume of Alex.

Madame Z began taking questions from the audience.

"William is opening up to me. He is honored by your presence and curious about your writing. What questions do you have for him?"

"Ask him why I didn't make the short list?" came a voice from the back of the room. Madame Z ignored the question.

"I see a hand up. Yes, the lady in the white blouse and overalls."

"I'm Scout; Scout Finch," she replied with frustration, as if she had spent the last hour or so explaining her costume. "I want to know what Faulkner's favorite book was, of all the novels he has written."

Madame Z closed her eyes and looked up at the paneled ceiling of the Queen Anne ballroom. Every eye in the room was on her as we held our breath during her pregnant pause.

"My cousin's favorite book, of all he has written, yes, William, yes, I will tell them. *The Old Man and the Sea!*"

The room exploded in outrage and the hackling of "You, filthy charlatan. Get out. Get out."

Suddenly, the gypsy band sprang into action with a very loud, very strange version of Mendelssohn's "Violin Concerto" as the wait staff ushered in the first course of dinner—hot French bread, butter, and marinated crab claws.

Ignatius finally began to speak by the second course, shrimp gumbo and a Creole tomato salad.

"Nobody gets it," he whispered next to me.

"Gets what?" I asked.

"Whom I'm supposed to be."

"I get it."

"So do I," reassured Matt.

"Maybe you should be holding a hot dog with a plastic squeeze bottle of mustard," offered Alex.

Ignatius stood up from the table, clutching his white, mouse-like hands. "It doesn't matter. It doesn't matter at all." He left the table, and after a while, I realized he wasn't coming back.

I picked up the cruet of oil and vinegar for the Creole tomato salad. "Salad dressing?"

Hemingway stared at me and the cruet for a while without answering.

For crying out loud, take the cruet. This isn't a moral decision.

The husband in the husband-and-wife team made love to the bread and butter; tenderly he tore a piece of bread from the loaf wrapped in a white linen napkin, then lavished it with butter.

"I'm Becky, Becky Lanier. My husband, Tom. Tom writes crime and mysteries, *The Bayou Black Series*. I write cookbooks.

"Interesting," I nodded, with a mouth full of blue crab. I swallowed hard and offered, "What do you like to cook?"

"Oh, I don't cook. Heavens no. Waaayyy too much work, standing in a hot kitchen all day. I like to eat, so I collect recipes of what I enjoy. I pay someone to cook for me."

"Oh, just like I wouldn't expect your husband to be a cop or a private investigator, because he writes mysteries."

"Yes, exactly. What do you write?"

"I write essays about drinking. But I'm an oddity. I actually drink then write about it."

Becky Lanier, cookbook author, smiled at me, revealing lettuce in her teeth.

"Want some bread, Karen?" Matt handed me the loaf and kicked me under the table.

"We come to the Quarter couple of times a year for plays and writing events. Can't wait to get back to Metairie where the Republicans live."

Suddenly, a loud clap of thunder sounded through the ballroom.

"That's Faulkner and he wants us to shut up," Matt offered.

"Summer squall from the Gulf." Hemingway finally had something to say. "These storms are frequent in July and August." I looked at him and saw a middle-aged man fishing Bimini in the stark white summer heat with his gaff and a club at his feet, waiting for the call of "Fish on."

The wait staff served the third course, Red Fish Pontchartrain. The sound of rain outside turned the conversation inward to the group at the table.

"Catfish Sonnier." Hemingway looked at us, extending his hand for a firm, manly shake.

"No, your name isn't Catfish." I touched the sleeve of the young man serving the plates. "Can we get some more wine here?"

"Karen, right? The birth certificate says Michael Sonnier. I'm a literate coon-ass from Algiers. I write travel journals. Creative essays. Got 7,500 views on my writer's blog."

"That's pirate country," Matt said, biting into the red fish stuffed with blue crab meat and gulf shrimp.

"I'm sure there's some in the family. I'm a car salesman by day and a writer by night. It's a good med for insomnia."

"Back to the name Catfish. I'm sure there's a story behind it."

"Of course, everybody's got a nickname in the South, and there's always a story behind it," Hemingway smiled. "I was fishing on the river with my cousins awhile back. Caught a big cat. Had a time getting the hook out of him. I didn't hold him just right and got stuck by the fin. Most people would use a pair of tweezers to get the needles out. I didn't have any. Used the point of a fish hook to dig it out. Cut myself up pretty good, and still didn't get it all out. Got poisoned by the fish spines. Hand swelled up, almost lost it."

I gave him a little pat on the back, "Well, you certainly deserve the moniker of Catfish."

The husband-and-wife team didn't respond. I'm sure they were wondering when this literary nightmare would be over and they could retreat to the gated neighborhoods and shopping malls of Metairie.

The fourth course arrived, Crème Brûlée served with chicory coffee, sugar and cream. Helen Songe, the founder of the Crescent City Literary Competition, and the Gertrude Stein of Southern writers, stepped up to the microphone.

"As I call your name, please join me on stage. We will begin with the novella category. First place, *A White Heat* by Joan Easterling. Second place, *Family Tradition* by Matthew Broussard. And third place, *A Fist Full of Nothing* by Melissa Carrington."

Ms. Songe placed a gold, silver, and platinum medal swinging on royal blue ribbons around the necks of the three writers. A photographer directed them to stand closer. From the audience, an anonymous female voice cried out, "Say cheese, y'all."

Chapter Thirty-five
O Little Flower

The French Quarter was fast asleep on Sunday morning as droplets of rain water fell from the white blooms of crepe myrtles in Jackson Square. Matt and I were walking hand-in-hand to St. Louis Cathedral. It was the city's most famous landmark with its triple steeples towering above the lacy iron galleries of the Pontalba Buildings. Saints and sinners had wept and pleaded with God in churches on this site for over three hundred years. What fires, hurricanes, and time destroyed, the faithful brought back, larger and grander.

I was overwhelmed by the emotion of going to church with Matt. I had spent so many years in and out of it, and most of those years spent on a back pew with old widowers with wrinkled clothes and sad eyes. Like me, they attended out of loneliness, habit and desperation. To enter the church with someone who knew my name, who sat next to me and prayed, brought me to tears. I hadn't known that simple comfort since the divorce.

Before we entered the nave, I saw a side altar to the right. I pulled Matt in the direction, where we found a carved enclave for St. Thérèse. In the alabaster marble of the Little Flower, with pink roses at her feet, I took a prayer card from a small wooden chair next to her and read it silently.

> *Give us the heart of a child who wonders*
> *at life and embraces everything with loving enthusiasm.*
> *Teach us your delight in God's ways,*

so that divine charity may blossom in our hearts.
Little Flower of Jesus, bring our petitions
before God, our Father.

I smiled at Matt standing next to me. "She was my confirmation saint when I was a little girl. I wanted to be as good as her when I was a kid. I failed miserably, but it's nice to remember that sentiment all those years ago."

"Just sentiment, Karen?"

"Yes, you're right. I've fought the church for years, but I always come back. I just find a peace here I can't find anywhere else."

"Let's go to Mass, Karen. It'll make both of us feel good."

"Deal."

"After Mass, I'll buy you some coffee and beignets and tell you about my wayward years as an altar boy."

We walked east along the cracked and broken sidewalks of Decatur. My airport tourist brochure stated the original Café Du Monde was built in the French Market, along the Mississippi River in 1862. I thought of the thousands of dock workers, shoppers, and merchants the café had served over the years. The plaque on the wall claimed the café only closed on Christmas Day and in the event of a hurricane.

We took a seat at a white round table beneath the friendly green-and-white striped canopy of the patio.

"What's your pleasure?" Matt pulled the aluminum chair closer to the table.

"I've never had a beignet. Let's get a big order. I love the idea of hot fried dough covered in powdered sugar and served with chicory coffee."

"Black coffee?"

"A little milk, please."

"You mean café au lait?"

There were few customers in the café. Most tourists were sleeping off Saturday night, and the locals were staying away until

Monday morning, when the tourists would leave with their plastic drink cups, made-in-China Mardi Gras masks, and miniature bottles of Creole hot sauce.

"I hate the thought of going home. Not that I don't love Tiffany and all, it's just been so great being with you. Actually, living in the moment. I've done so little of that." I poured a bit of milk into my coffee and took a deep drink. The smell was of sweet tobacco, but the taste was acrid, almost woody. Even in the early morning heat and humidity of July, it was satisfying.

"It's been quite a weekend, Karen. A roller coaster ride, really." He laughed into his coffee cup and looked at me. "I want more of these weekends. I want more of you." He stood up from his chair and kissed me across the table.

"I do, too, but I don't see how. There's school, the baby coming . . . I don't know when I'll be able to get away again."

"Karen, we don't have to go away together. We can live our lives, together. I know that's a crap shoot with a guy that's been married three times, but remember, technically, I've only been married twice. You can't hold it against me."

"What are you saying?" *Is this a shack-up request or a weak marriage proposal?*

"I know it's quick, but after my MFA is complete, I hope to build a house in Mountain Home. I've got some land there. We can live there. Together."

"Mountain Home? Where? I don't know what you're saying. Do you want a roommate? An editor for your writing?" What are you telling me?" I took a huge bite of the beignet, and the powdered sugar exploded on the front of my dress.

"Mountain Home is about an hour west of Kerrville. It's remote, but beautiful. We could have a nice life there, as a couple, married, if that's what you want."

"What about Tiffany, the baby, my job? I can't just move to the wilds of Central Texas and be your house frau."

"Karen, slow down. Just think about it. We can do it a step at a time. Tiffany and her baby would be welcome. I want that with you. All of it. But let's do it slowly. You need to breathe. I can hear your heart pounding from here. Your ear lobes are resting on your shoulders. Settle down."

"I don't know. I just don't know." I looked away from him and studied the people walking back and forth in the market, setting their wares out for the day, tee shirts with glittery fleur-de-lis symbols, fruit, vegetables, keychains with attached shrunken alligator heads, tie-dyed scarves, and Jazz CDs—a gumbo of memorabilia from the melting pot of the Mississippi.

"Hey." He reached across the table and took my hand. "One step at a time."

"Okay." I couldn't look at him. Instead, I looked at the spray of white sugar on the bodice of my black sundress.

"What time does your plane leave?"

"2:00 p.m."

"Let's get back to the hotel. I'll call a cab for you." He stood up, placed a twenty-dollar bill on the table, and walked away. I immediately ran after him.

The plane sat on the tarmac for thirty minutes before the flight attendants began closing the overhead bins and instructing us how to save our lives and those around us if we crashed into the Gulf of Mexico.

Part animal and poor deodorant choice, the smell coming from the woman sitting next to me quickly became overpowering. I gave a careful side glance at her. Typical frosted and layered bob haircut of the middle-aged professional woman. She was sweating profusely as she sponged her neck and forehead with a very tired paper napkin.

She smiled at me. "I'm going home for the first time in six weeks. Got this new job. Dream job with great money, but the traveling is killing me."

She picked up her cell phone from her lap and began texting furiously as the plane was taxiing off the runway. She stopped, wiped her brow, and threw the phone in her purse.

"My sixteen-year-old. We barely speak, but that can be a

good thing," She laughed at herself, breathlessly. "Giving him the two-hour warning. I'll be home soon."

I smiled at her to be polite and settled into my seat. I stared at the back of heads before me until I closed my eyes. I thought about how I use to parent Tiffany. I thought a text now and then would make it all okay. It didn't. Living my life through a routine of working, texting, and drinking . . . it wasn't living. It was existing.

I'm going to marry Matt Broussard, and I'm going to love being a grandma to Tiffany's baby. Despite the odds, despite all the brokenness of each of us, we're going to be a family. I'm not going to forget to do some living this time around.

Chapter Thirty-six
A Death in the Family

On the fifth of August, I awoke to an emptiness within me, a profound sorrow I hadn't felt since losing my parents. I sat on the edge of the bed, unconscious to the morning light and Max sleeping on the floor. I knew. I knew she was gone.

I didn't put on a robe but ran across the street in my nightgown; my bare feet wet from the morning's dew. I ran to the house with the picture window and the manicured lawn. I ran past the zinnias, purple and hot pink in the flowerbed under the ornamental pear tree. I stopped running and stood in front of the door with its handmade wreath of plastic flowers and ribbons.

The door was unlocked. I called her name before walking in. I didn't expect her to answer. I was simply delaying the shock of what I'd find within.

"Leona. Leona."

I found her on the kitchen floor. She was wearing a snap-front house dress in pastel stripes and pink slippers on her feet. In her hand was a spatula. The water was running in the kitchen sink. On the counter was a floured cake pan.

I laid next to her on the black-and-white tile floor. I put my ear next to her heart. Nothing. Her chest never rose again to accept a rush of oxygen. The inhale and exhale of life was stopped by a heart attack.

"Oh Leona. My sweet, sweet Leona. My friend." I held her

and wept bitterly on the floor next to her. I didn't cry for her. I cried for me. I would have to live my life every day without her. I had needed her far more than she ever needed me.

She died alone, as alone as she had lived most of her life; the little Hungarian girl trapped in an adult body that carried the tales of a childhood robbed of its promise and innocence. She bore a sorrow few knew and even fewer dared to understand.

But grief is buried temporarily in the rituals of burying the dead. The only living relative of Leona's I could find was a cousin who lived in Minnesota. The old woman was too fragile to survive the flight to Houston; the thought of officiating at the funeral of her last relative to share her name and history was unbearable.

On August eighth Father Patrick O'Connor of St. Thérèse Catholic Church blessed the casket holding Leona Molnar Supak with holy water. I thought of the waters of baptism she received as an infant in St. Stephen's Basilica in Budapest eighty-one years ago.

I placed the white pall over her casket thinking of the white of her First Communion dress. Her Rosary Beads and a prayer book were placed on top of the white cloth. I had found them on a nightstand in her bedroom the night she died.

I walked with the casket to the altar. I didn't deserve that privilege. I was only there by default.

Father O'Connor spoke of a life well-lived in service and devotion to the church, closing the homily with a prayer Leona had prayed so often in her life.

> The Lord is my shepherd; I shall not want.
> He makes me lie down in green pastures;
> He leads me beside still waters; he restores my soul.
> He leads me in right paths for his name's sake.

> Even though I walk through the darkest valley,
> I fear no evil; for you are with me;
> your rod and your staff—they comfort me.

You prepare a table before me
in the presence of my enemies;
you anoint my head with oil;
my cup overflows.

Surely goodness and mercy
shall follow me all the days of my life,
and I shall dwell in the house
of the Lord my whole life long.

Tiffany slumped on one side of me, with Matt on the other side. They each held my hand, and I cried out of shame, out of humility, out of selfishness, out of love for a woman I hardly knew. Tiffany sobbed by my side, swiping her nose and eyes with a white, embroidered handkerchief Leona had made for her. With a patient and careful hand, Leona had stitched a little pink rose with the initials T.A. *Sweet, dear Tiffany. Another person you love has said goodbye. This is the sad reality of our lives, honey. We will spend a life time saying goodbye to people we love, slowly learning how to live without them.* I put my arm around her, and she laid her head against my shoulder.

Behind us sat Kelly and Carl. Kelly was dressed in a solemn black dress with a white Peter Pan collar. Of course, I couldn't see her shoes from where I was sitting. They could be pink combat boots, who knew? Who cared? I was glad she was here. She and Leona weren't the best of friends, but I knew Kelly respected her. How could you not? Leona was a one-in-a-million woman who could work like a man and still look like a woman. Elegant Leona, like the beautiful strand of pearls she always wore. Classic. Refined. Rare. Carl offered me a sad smile. *Carl, you were a good friend to her.*

On a pew in the back sat Greg and Barbara. Tiffany must have called them. It was very decent of them to come. Tiffany and Greg had become closer since he took on the legal charges against Jared. He occasionally picked her up and took her to lunch while I was at work. It was good for the both of them. I don't know if Barbara knew about their lunches. It was probably best for all if that was kept secret. To make Barbara jealous would only end the lunches Greg and Tiffany shared; but more importantly, it would sever the tender friendship they had finally found.

Joan Simons and Martha Garza, Leona's devoted friends she had served with in the St. Thérèse Altar Society, carried the Gifts to the altar, dressed in black pantsuits, Joan with a ruffled blouse, while Martha chose a red polyester blouse with a simple collar. I had met them many times in Leona's kitchen, drinking coffee and eating pastries Leona had just pulled from the oven. They never invited me to join them.

They were a secret, exclusive society, a friendship of over forty years, as the heartaches and joys of life, the rising and falling of emotion, was steadied through the years by their love for each other and their faith. The Altar Society Ladies of St. Thérèse never asked me to join them, because they knew my faith was infantile. Instead, they prayed for me.

Following Communion, Father O'Connor blessed the coffin with incense. "In peace let us take our sister, Leona Molnar Supak to her place of rest." He made the sign of the cross. "Following the burial, please join us at the home of Karen Anders for food and fellowship. There's a printed invitation in the narthex with directions to Karen's house."

Every pastry, cake, sweet roll, and coffee cake served at Leona's wake was store-bought. She would have hated that, but secretly, she would have loved it, knowing her culinary skills would never be matched by any American, let alone a girl-woman from Houston, Texas. Leona's peers were the European gentry taught by their mothers, who worked for the royal houses of the rich and privileged. With nimble fingers, they created light textured miracles from flour, butter, eggs, and sugar.

"For God's sake, Kelly, don't lick the serving spoon before placing it back in the dish. Pull your dress down; this is a wake, not a cocktail bar. Carl, can you take care of trash duty?"

"I'm going to forget you said that and recognize your nasty

remark as a form of crippling grief." Kelly pulled her dress down to her knees and placed the pasta salad on the dining room table.

"Do you want a garbage can in the dining room? Makes it a lot easier for people."

"No, Carl, just pick up the plates and cups around the area, throw them in the garbage in here. Oh yeah, make sure Max isn't looking for table scraps while people are trying to eat." Carl walked away dutifully.

"You want me to carve the ham?"

"Thank God you're here, Matt. Did I really just have to explain to Carl that an open container of trash would not be appropriate next to the dining room table? I'm exhausted and we haven't even started. Look, there's a carving knife in here." I pointed to the cabinet drawer, watching Tiffany stroke her huge belly as she sat on the couch in the living room. "Is she okay?"

"Is who okay?"

"Tiffany's been rubbing her stomach since we got back from the cemetery."

"What pregnant woman is not miserable in August? She's okay."

"Do this for me. Make sure Barbara and my ex don't come into this kitchen. This is a house we used to share. I don't want her eye-balling things, making me a nervous wreck."

"I don't think you're going to get any kitchen help from those two. They're interesting to watch, though. He brings her an hors d'oeuvre; she rolls her eyes. He gets her something to drink; she rolls her eyes. He's here for you and Tiffany. That's quite a compliment to the both of you. It's obvious he had to drag her here, kicking and screaming."

The wake buffet was arranged on the table with a vase of white tulips, the national flower of Hungary, in the center. Matt bought them from a florist in River Oaks. I'm sure he paid a fortune for them. The delicate, pristine flowers were in sharp contrast to the humble marigolds and zinnias I had potted on the front porch. I was surprised they were still alive in this heat.

Father O'Connor rose from the couch, where he had sat with Tiffany, and addressed the small gathering.

"Thank you for the beautiful food, Karen. Let's pray. Bless us, O Lord, and these Thy gifts, which we are about to receive from Thy bounty through Christ Our Lord, Amen."

Of all the human rituals, through all the ages, nothing is more comforting to me than people gathered around a table, praying, eating, and talking. It's why Thanksgiving and Christmas meant more to me than other holidays. All I could think was how pleased Leona would have been. I looked at Martha and Joan, the altar society ladies, and they smiled back at me.

I walked into the kitchen to bring out another pitcher of iced tea; Tiffany followed me in.

"I just peed in my pants."

"You just peed in your pants? Are you sure you just didn't spill something in your lap, Tiffany? It's hard to be this pregnant, plus all the emotion of the day."

"No, I peed in my pants."

"Her water broke," Matt said behind us.

Tiffany started crying and I grabbed my purse.

"Matt, drive. I'll sit in the back with her."

"Now Karen, this might be a bit premature. We might wait until the contractions become stronger."

Tiffany greeted that statement with a wail. "I want to go now! Now, the hospital!"

"Matt, you're driving. Get the suitcase. Tiffany, put some clean underwear on and a big sundress. Nothing around your waist, sweetie. Let's go."

I entered the dining room adjoined by a half wall into the living room and made the announcement.

"Tiffany's water broke. Y'all stay here and eat."

"Oh honey, how exciting!" Joan clapped on the couch.

Father O'Connor placed his hand on Tiffany's head, "God bless you, Tiffany. You're in good hands. We'll be praying for you and the baby."

"We'll get the kitchen for you, Karen. Be here when you come back," Martha offered.

"Call us as soon as y'all hear something," Kelly gave Tiffany a hug. Carl stood next to her holding a white kitchen garbage bag.

Greg approached me, whispering in my ear. "For legal matters, you need to think about whose name will be representing the father on that birth certificate."

"Shut up, Greg." I walked toward the front door, stepping on Poncho's tail. Poor cat. Without a sound, he scurried under the couch. It was the safest place to be amid the chaos. "Carl, make sure Poncho's okay," I yelled from the open door. "Give him a can of tuna for supper and extra cheese slices for Max. This has been a hard day for them too."

Matt had the AC blowing in the Jeep. With her face bent toward the air duct, Tiffany sat in the back seat, fanning her red face and neck. I dragged the safety belt across me as he backed up, hitting a huge garbage bag Carl had placed on the curb.

"Forget it. Just keep driving." I pulled my hair into a tight ponytail with a rubber band I found in the cup holder, then turned around to the back seat to rub Tiffany's bent shoulders.

"This baby won't have a daddy. Just like me. Just like me," Tiffany cried, her tears running along her face, mixing with the sweat beading on her neck.

"Honey, it's the twenty-first century and most kids don't have a daddy living with them. It's just a sad truth, but I'm here; Matt's here. That constitutes a family. We're going to love and take care of each other, especially this baby."

A baby girl arrived at 4:00 p.m. the following evening. She weighed six pounds and eleven ounces. Her height was measured at seventeen inches. With black hair and blue eyes, she had all her fingers and toes. She carried the name of a woman who was faithful and strong, Leona Aliz Anders.

One life ended and another began.

Chapter Thirty-seven
Bulletproof

I didn't know at the time; I was going through each day and night, like a mad woman, taking care of Tiffany and Leona Aliz, teaching and grading, shopping and cleaning. I didn't have time to drink. I didn't want to drink. The anxiety quilled by alcohol was replaced by the simplest, sweetest realization. I was needed.

Matt was there. Steady. Self-assuring. Here for a week, a weekend, he was always coming and going, graduating with a MFA, writing another novel, and placing an engagement ring with a solitary pearl on my finger.

It was happening all around me. A family was being formed. We were living for each other—Tiffany, the baby, Matt, and me. It wasn't something we planned; it happened. Strangers and disappointments came together and made a home for four human beings. The bond was that darling baby girl, Leona Aliz. She saved us; saved us from a bottle, a broken heart, and loneliness. Like her namesake, my dear Leona, they made us the best we could be, individually. Together, we were bulletproof.

Some women may be crushed by the thought of being called grandma. As if the name made you an old woman overnight. Like most labels, it was just a buy-in to accept what others thought of you. The only label I ever took seriously was American girl-woman. It hurt me, but Leona was right. She was the first friend to demand more of me, because she believed I was capable of more.

Leona Aliz made me a better woman. A granddaughter was

different than a daughter, because I was different. I was smarter than the newly divorced woman juggling a job and a baby.

I often thought of things Leona Supak shared with me. The things she taught me without me realizing it at the time. The most beautiful gift I received from her was realizing love, friendship, food and family were extraordinary blessings, never to be reduced to common, trivial assumptions that the living, life itself, would always be waiting there for us. The heartbreaking assumption we had all the time in the world and we could pick and choose when to love and when to hold was gone with a hard-fast truth. All of it could disappear, the family, the husband, the child, the home, food . . . all of it could disappear in a heartbeat. This was a world where change should be expected, and with it the sorrow that we continue despite the change. Leona taught me well. It was how I came to be a mother, grandmother, and a wife.

Leona's house came up for sale and a young family bought it. I made a Hungarian coffee cake with nuts and plums and carried it across the street. A pogo stick and a bright yellow miniature dump trunk replaced the Shepherd's Hook that once held Leona's marigolds, zinnias, and angel-wing begonias. The wreath was gone from the front door. Behind it, the voice of a woman and two children running through the house, could be heard above the ringing of the doorbell.

"Hi, I'm your neighbor, Karen, across the street. Welcome to the neighborhood."

A chestnut brunette in her late thirties smiled at me. Two boys, a toddler and a preschooler, appeared at the door behind their mother. The toddler hung on to his mother's pant leg.

"Hi. I'm Sarah. My boys, Sean and Henry. Come in. Oh, my gosh, this looks incredible." She took the coffee cake from me.

"Not this time. I know you're busy. I just wanted to introduce myself. Hello there, Sean and Henry. Let me know if you need anything. It's a great neighborhood. I've been here a long time. Lots of friendly people. Very safe."

"I appreciate that." Sarah smiled at me. "Hey, boys, what do we say?"

A chorus rang out, "Thank you."

"I'll get your plate back to you. Maybe coffee then?"

"Sure." I smiled and walked back across the street. I had done it so often over the years, walking back and forth from Leona's house to mine. Sometimes I was drunk; sometimes I was crying; many times, I was terribly alone, but this time I was Karen, Leona Aliz's grandmother, and that was the very best thing of all.

"How are the new neighbors?" Tiffany shouted from the kitchen table.

"Young family. Very sweet." I walked into the kitchen and sat next to her. Leona Aliz was asleep in the bouncy chair on the kitchen table. A stack of textbooks and highlighters surrounded both of them.

"Homework for class?" I asked Tiffany, as I gently rubbed the soles of the baby's bare feet with my index finger.

"The cloze reading test for children. Pretty cool. You can determine a reading level by the number of words and syllables in a sentence. This will come in handy when doing lesson plans."

"You got the bug all right! Never thought you'd want to be a teacher, so glad for both you and the baby. It's a good career. Summers off. Won't get rich being in the education business, but your work will mean something."

Tiffany closed her book and put the cap on her highlighter.

"I learned a lot from living with a teacher. The best she had to give me." She stood up and gave me a hug.

Yes, it happened, just like the building of a family where there was none. The most marvelous thing occurred along the way. Tiffany became a mother and I became a grandmother, and in that, we became friends.

"What do you want for supper?"

"Taco Tuesday! I'll make guacamole. Better get the homework done while the baby's napping. I'll help when I'm done." She gathered her book and backpack and walked into the living room to read. She was still too thin, but maybe that's the way it always would be. Max looked up from the kitchen floor and followed her into the living room, jumping onto the couch next to her. Poncho was asleep in the chair next to them.

Yes, it was happening all around me. I had a beautiful life.

Chapter Thirty-eight
The Hope Diamond

The early morning chill and the smell of oak leaves enveloped us on the porch as we sipped coffee together. It was our morning ritual in Mountain Home, to share the first cup of coffee for the day before separating to our individual writing desks in the cabin.

When we moved here a year ago, I came as a fifty-five-year-old bride, grandmother, and retired teacher. Living on 270 acres in a 1,500-square foot cabin in Central Texas with a man who lost a foot in the Middle East and two wives in-between was foolhardy to say the least. Despite the odds, we've made a good life for ourselves, as well as for Tiffany and Leona Aliz.

"Do I Dare?" wept Prufrock. *Yes, I do.* I leaped forward with arms spread wide open. I'd let my hair gray, my guard down, and crawled into bed with Matt Broussard, with a simple gold band symbolizing our faith in each other.

Tiffany teaches third grade at Dobie Elementary in Kerrville; Leona Aliz attends the pre-K program while her mother works. My daughter is long-legged and battle-scared. The dark shadow of self-doubt follows her closely. She is a loving mother and a caring teacher, despite the insecurities of abandonment courtesy of Jared and her birth mother. The breaking of her heart and the emptiness of being would visit her again, like it will for each of us, despite our silent vow to be smarter the next time around.

But Leona Aliz, Tiffany's only child, was Heaven in motion with thick black hair and blue eyes. Her youth, her complete joy in the ordinary day, almost healed Tiffany from the things that never came true for her. The names Jared and Sherry, the monikers of first love and mother are words rarely spoken out loud by Tiffany, but they're there in her head, sloshing around. They became part of something within her, she never quite got over. It is how Tiffany came to be Tiffany.

My ex and his wife have three children now. It would seem the surrogate route worked well for a couple who wanted it all. I get a Christmas card every year with a picture of the five of them posed in front of an iconic vacation spot somewhere in the world. The sentiment and the signature on the card are simple: Happy Holidays from the Denison Family. Every year I have the same reaction when I get the card—*I used to love him a long time ago.*

All buttoned-up, zipped, a perfectly aligned life, was everyone's life on Facebook and the holiday photo card. It's phony, but everyone is afraid to say it out loud. There's all that shame and regret to bind you about the shoulders and neck, like a Puritan in a rack. It's best not to be too candid with 2,700 Facebook friends you've never met.

Life is messy. Families are messy. Some days we're off track, just like every other family in the world. We're trying to stay afloat in the same life boat. No one can bail out in a storm, least we all go overboard. It's just what we do to survive, even on the good days.

"You want another cup, birthday girl?" Matt stood up and walked toward the house. I knew he was done with the quiet of the morning between us. He wanted to write, before that scene, that perfect first sentence was gone in his head, before that first bolt of caffeine lost its punch.

"You had to remind me about the birthday. Tiffany was the first reminder. She left a card on the kitchen table." I stood up, handing my coffee cup to him. "No more coffee for me. I'm walking this morning. I'll check the mailbox at the road." He smiled and walked into the house. And that is where he would stay until noon, writing and rewriting.

Matt won the PEN/Faulkner award for his second novel *Atchafalaya River Song* in June and was filled with the need to make the next book even better. It was a curse. The more he wrote, the more he wanted to write. I was happy to write a column for the *Mountain Home Weekly Gazette*. It was the last of the few small-town weeklies. I make a whopping $25 a column. That was enough for me.

I began my walk on the west side of the property. I had a coveted route for my destination since I had moved here, marking my way with coffee cups I had left out in earlier walks or tying a colorful rag to a tree limb. Sometimes I'd take Leona Aliz with me and we'd talk about the different flowers, names of trees, and types of birds as we walked. I wanted her to know that. I wanted her to know so many things.

The November weather made it almost a religious pilgrimage through the hilly grass lands of the Edwards Plateau. My boots crunched the dry switchgrass beneath me. The land was not completely cleared of the heavy mesquite brush and dead cedar. Matt's denim jacket protected my arms and shoulders from the underbrush.

After an hour's walk, I found the large limestone rock I had made my spot in the walks since moving here. This is where I came to think and pray. A church made from God's handiwork of white limestone, juniper bushes, and wilted bellflowers, with their tiny blue flowers faded as late fall prepared the land for winter. The quail in the low grasses, the sound of the mockingbirds in the scrub oak, were a chorus in the perfect orchestra of nature. Occasionally, a family of javelina or a white-tailed deer would walk across the little opening, if I were still and quiet. A herd of wild turkey hens and their chicks foraged in the ground for berries and seed not far from me. In that perfect quiet I could hear the wind push through the wings of a hawk flying above my head.

Near this rock we buried Poncho and Max underneath a cottonwood tree. There wasn't a day gone by I didn't think of them, Leona, and my family. That life can begin and end in such a rapid-fire succession never stopped being a shock for me. I never matured from the sensitive young woman who lost her family and failed in her first marriage. That was the noise that sloshed in my head.

Matt had been right about Mountain Home. This life, this land, gave me a foundation I never found in Houston; it allowed me to control the demon in the wine bottle, that rose and fell with my anxiety, reminding me I am who I am. There were better days since we moved here.

I reflected on another birthday, the growing number of candles on the cake, and the wishes that come and go with each year. The bright morning star stood in the blue sky above me. I watched it for a long time and thought of a Psalm my grandmother often recited, "Create in me a pure heart, O God, and renew a steadfast spirit within me." I took the birthday card out of my back pocket. A letter was folded inside the card.

Dear Karen,

I wanted to wish you more than a happy birthday. I want to thank you for always being there.
Always. When Dad died and my mother left, you
were there. When high school and girl drama ruled,
you were there. When I didn't even love myself,
you never stopped loving me. You just never quit,
even when I quit you. I see my life now, with
Leona Aliz, dating again, a real job. It's how I came
to be. Not who I was, but the person you knew
I could be. You always saw the Hope Diamond
when you looked at me. Your Tiffany. In time, you
made me believe it, too. Maybe that's how it was
meant to be for all of us, from where we started
to how we came to be. You made it possible.

I love you,
Tiffany

About the Author

A former English teacher and journalist, Johnnie Bernhard's passion is reading and writing. She is an award-winning author of nonfiction and fiction.

Her work(s) have appeared in the following publications: *University of Michigan Graduate Studies Publications, Heart of Ann Arbor Magazine, Houston Style Magazine, World Oil Magazine, The Suburban Reporter of Houston, The Mississippi Press, University of South Florida Area Health Education Magazine,* the international *Word Among Us, Southern Writers Magazine, Texas Review Magazine, Southern Literary Review,* and the Cowbird-NPR production on small town America. Her entry, "The Last Mayberry," received over 7,500 views, nationally and internationally.

Her debut novel, *A Good Girl,* was short listed in the 2015 William Faulkner-William Wisdom Creative Writing Competition. Published by Texas Review Press, it was a 2017 featured novel for panel discussion at the Mississippi and Louisiana Book Festivals, as well as a finalist in the 2017 Kindle Book Awards. For more about *A Good Girl,* please visit the author's website at www.johnniebernhardauthor.com.

How We Came to Be is Johnnie's second novel. It was a finalist in the 2017 Faulkner-Wisdom Writing Competition.

Lightning Source UK Ltd.
Milton Keynes UK
UKHW01f2012080918
328553UK00002B/129/P

9 781680 031560